*Wishbone caught sight
of the evil-looking,
long, black limo. . . .*

The sleek car cruised silently down the road in front of the drive-in. It didn't stop or slow down, but it passed by three times.

Wishbone knew in his canine heart that if the limo was there, then scary Harry Bliss must be seated inside, smiling his cold smile. Wishbone shuddered, as if a gust of cold, wet autumn wind had suddenly blown across the drive-in lot. "Harry Bliss. Now, *there's* a sinister guy."

Wishbone looked around.

"Gotta keep an eye out so I can warn Joe if that man does anything . . . uh . . . scary."

Other books in the
WISHBONE™ Mysteries series:

WISHBONE Mysteries

DRIVE-IN OF DOOM

by Brad Strickland and Thomas E. Fuller

WISHBONE™ created by Rick Duffield

Big Red Chair Books™, *A Division of **Lyrick Publishing**™*

This book is a work of fiction. The characters, incidents, and dialogues are products of the authors' imagination and are not to be construed as real. Any resemblance to actual events or persons, living or dead, is entirely coincidental.

 Big Red Chair Books™, *A Division of Lyrick Publishing*™
300 E. Bethany Drive, Allen, Texas 75002

©1998 Big Feats! Entertainment

Edited by Kevin Ryan

Copy edited by Jonathon Brodman

Cover concept and design by Lyle Miller

Interior illustrations by Kathryn Yingling

Wishbone photograph by Carol Kaelson

Library of Congress Catalog Card Number: 97-75678

ISBN: 1-57064-282-6

First printing: April 1998

10 9 8 7 6 5 4 3 2 1

Printed in the United States of America

To Amy, who's always at home in the theater
                    —Brad Strickland

To my favorite nephews, Benjamin and Sam Scott,
           who will love drive-ins
         as much as Wishbone does—
     as soon as they're old enough to go
                    —Thomas E. Fuller

FROM THE BIG RED CHAIR . . .

Oh . . . hi! Wishbone here. You caught me right in the middle of some of my favorite things—books. Let me welcome you to the WISHBONE MYSTERIES. In each story, I help my human friends solve a puzzling mystery. In **DRIVE-IN OF DOOM**, the local drive-in movie theater is being vandalized. My pal Joe and I are on the case, and we hope to stop the culprit before the drive-in is destroyed!

The story takes place late in the summer, during the same time period as the events you'll see in the second season of my WISHBONE television show. In this story, Joe is fourteen, and he and his friends are about to enter the eighth grade. Like me, they are always ready for adventure . . . and a good mystery.

You're in for a real treat, so pull up a chair and a snack and sink your teeth into **DRIVE-IN OF DOOM**.

Chapter One

J oe Talbot stepped out of his house, adjusted his black-leather jacket over his white T-shirt, and ran a comb through his slicked-back brown hair. He flicked open a pair of sunglasses, put them on, and swaggered to the sidewalk, his biker boots clacking on the pavement.

Wishbone, a white-with-brown-and-black-spots Jack Russell terrier, trotted beside his best friend as Joe headed downtown. *Hmm . . . there's something different about today,* Wishbone thought as they hurried along. *Let's see, nice warm Saturday morning at the end of summer, sort of lazy— Nope, I just can't put my paw on it, but something is definitely different.*

Wrinkling his forehead in thought, Wishbone looked at his friend. Joe Talbot was fourteen years old, athletic, and usually a cheerful guy. Well, Wishbone decided, that hadn't changed. Joe grinned as he strode along, the August late-morning sunlight reflecting brightly off his shades. He looked down and said, "Come on, buddy. Race you to the corner!"

Wishbone's tongue wagged in anticipation. "You're on! Ready—set—*I'm outta here!*"

The two ran full-tilt down the sidewalk. With his four legs, Wishbone could easily outdistance Joe, but he held himself back enough so the good-natured race ended in a draw. He pulled up short at the corner and stared toward the main street of Oakdale.

"Whoa! I was right! Today *is* different! Just look at that!"

Oakdale's downtown shopping district had been decorated for some special occasion. Strings of triangular pennants swung from lamppost to lamppost. Every store had a big, colorful banner tacked up on its front. Crowds of people were gathered in the streets, and—Wishbone's nose twitched in eager anticipation—there was lots of food! Someone was cooking food! Loads of it, and many different kinds. Wishbone could pick out the individual aroma of hot dogs, hamburgers, pizzas, cookies, cakes, ice cream— a feast!

"Wow!" Joe said. "I guess Fabulous Fifties Day is a success. Just look at that, Wishbone."

Wishbone sniffed again. "*Look?* Take a deep sniff, Joe! I don't know what Fabulous Fifties Day is, but it smells great!"

"Come on," Joe said. "I told Sam and David we'd meet them at the hot-dog stand over by Rosie's."

Wishbone licked his chops. "Hot dogs? Hot dog! Joe, you're the greatest! Race you there!"

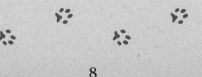

At first, Joe had felt a little self-conscious. His fifties costume consisted of thrift-shop jeans, their legs almost too tight for him to move comfortably. Along with the black-leather jacket, he wore biker boots and a skintight T-shirt. He had applied lots of hair tonic, too. Now he was the image of a tough kid right out of a 1950s movie. Wishbone had come along as his pet, though of course Wishbone didn't have to change *his* costume to be in style.

Joe swaggered down the street, hoping that he looked as cool as he felt. Some of the other boys had also slicked their hair back with hair tonic, but most of them were just wearing flannel shirts, jeans, and sneakers. Joe really stood out from the crowd.

He stepped around the tree outside Rosie's Rendezvous Books & Gifts and grinned. His close friends David Barnes and Samantha Kepler had already arrived. David had dressed as a bookworm. He was wearing black horn-rimmed glasses (but with no lenses, Joe noticed), a white-nylon shirt with a pocket protector filled with lots of pens, and black slacks that were slightly short. Clipped to his belt was a long brown rectangular box made of leather, looking something like a holster.

Sam looked right on target in her outfit. She had pulled her blond hair back into a floppy ponytail. She wore a white blouse and a long, full gray skirt with a white-and-black poodle design on it. Sam wore rolled-down white socks—the type once called bobby socks. Completing her outfit were white shoes with a black saddle-shaped patch of leather sewn over the insteps. Sam had told David these were called black-and-white saddle Oxfords.

Sam and David caught sight of Joe and Wishbone and waved them over.

"Hi," Joe said, coming up to them. "Sam, you look neat!"

"Thanks, Daddy-o," Sam replied with a grin. "Hi, Wishbone! How are you doing?" Sam leaned over and gave Wishbone's head and ears a good, long scratch. Judging from Wishbone's pleased expression, Joe thought the Jack Russell terrier enjoyed the attention. Wishbone had his eyes squeezed shut, his tongue hanging out, and his mouth open in a big doggie grin.

"Daddy-o?" Joe asked David.

David shrugged. "Don't look at me. She's been talking like that all day. I guess you're a juvenile delinquent, huh?"

"I'm just a cool dude who—"

"Cat!" Sam corrected with a laugh. Wishbone looked up sharply, and Sam continued. "In the fifties, dudes were easterners who dressed up like cowboys. You'd have been a cool *cat* back then."

Trying to look serious, Joe said, "I'm a cool . . . uh . . . *cat* who—digs?"

"'Digs' is good," Sam said.

"Who digs hot cars," Joe finished. "What's in the holster?"

Grinning, David opened the leather container and pulled out something that looked like a very thick, wide ruler. It was in three sections, and the middle section slid back and forth. "My retro computer," David said.

"What is it?" Joe asked.

Laughing, David said, "It's called a slide rule. And back before transistors and microchips, students had to

10

use them to make calculations. This once belonged to my grandfather."

"People had it rough back then," Joe said, wondering how in the world anyone could calculate anything on the contraption. "Guys, to tell you the truth, I'm glad we don't live in the fifties."

Sam twirled around, making her skirt flare out. "Don't be a square, Joe. Get hep. Get into the swing of things. This is Fabulous Fifties Day, remember?"

"Oh, I get it," Joe said. "Uh . . . far out. Groovy."

Sam nearly collapsed with laughter. "Sorry, Joe. Those words are from the seventies, I think. I guess I'll have to give you some language lessons—that is, if you want to be cool."

"Teach us after lunch," David said. "I'm starved. Hey, Joe, come on over to the hot-dog stand with us. You won't believe the fifties prices!"

Wishbone's ears perked up and his mouth watered when David mentioned lunch. He looked up with approval. "I'm with David, Joe! And I'm with Sam, too! *I* want to be cool. And what could be cooler than a cool dog like me eating a hot dog like— Whoa! Like one of those I smell!"

They had walked past the boutique to a spot on the sidewalk where a hot-dog vendor had set up his wagon. Above the wagon, two poles supported a banner that fluttered in the breeze. It showed the freckled face of a red-haired boy, and red, white, and blue letters spelled out a message.

Joe read the words aloud: "'Howdy Doody Hot-Dog Stand.' Who's Howdy Doody?"

"Now, *that* I know," replied David as the four got in line. "Sam may be the language expert, but I know the TV shows and the music from the fifties. Old Howdy was a world-famous puppet who had his very own children's television show. He was a star!"

"Star of his own show?" Wishbone said. "Wow!" Wishbone's nose twitched, and he kept licking his chops. "Well, howdy, Howdy! Oh, that smell is driving me crazy!" He pawed Joe's leg to get his attention. "How about a snack, buddy?"

David bought a hot dog, a soft drink, and a bag of chips. "That will be fifteen cents," said the cheerful hot-dog-stand owner, a young man in a white hat and white apron.

"Is that all?" Joe asked.

The young man winked. "Fifties prices for today only," he replied.

Sam and Joe bought their own hot dogs, and Joe bought an extra one for Wishbone. Wishbone ate his in a couple of gulps, then watched as the others dressed theirs up with onion, relish, mustard, and ketchup.

"This is a great idea," David announced as he expertly squirted a squiggly yellow line of mustard across the top of his hot dog. "Can you imagine what it must have been like to be a kid in the fifties? If I'd been alive back then and had the same allowance I have today, I'd be rich!"

Wishbone gave up begging and studied Sam's costume thoughtfully. "Nice picture of a poodle you have there, Sam. Reminds me of someone I know from across town." Wishbone yawned. "Oh, well, I'll just settle down here beside Joe. If you happen to have any scraps left over from lunch, remember Wishbone's Cheerful Disposal Service!"

Joe had a little bit of bun and a small piece of hot dog left when he finished his lunch, and he tossed them to Wishbone, who caught the edible treasure on the fly. Joe couldn't help but laugh. "You know," he said to David and Sam, "if baseball were played with meatballs, Wishbone would be a great center fielder."

David grinned at him. "He would be named Most Valuable Player."

"Get hep," Sam said again. "Like, the Food Olympics, dig? That would be real gone."

Joe wondered what she was talking about. Before

he could ask, a blaring car horn jerked his attention away from Sam and toward the street, where a deep blue auto glided past. "Wow!" he said. "The antique cars are here. Look at that!"

David whistled. "Is that a Ford?"

Joe shook his head. "No, it's a 1948 Packard, and it's a real beauty."

Sam smoothed her skirt. "The Antique Car Club was the reason for Fabulous Fifties Day, right?"

"That's right," Joe said. "When the state Antique Car Club announced it was having its summer convention in Oakdale, the Oakdale Historical Society came up with the idea of having Fabulous Fifties Day to help celebrate the occasion. I think Miss Gilmore has joined the club, too—you know how proud she is of her 1957 Thunderbird. Hey, look at that 1956 two-tone Chevy. That's a neat car!"

The antique auto had a two-color paint job of aqua and cream, and its chrome gleamed in the bright sunshine. It was a convertible, with the top down. As the well-preserved auto cruised grandly down Main Street at a speed of five to ten miles an hour, a woman in the backseat clutched a broad-brimmed purple hat to her head and waved enthusiastically.

"Hey!" Sam said. "That's Miss Gilmore."

Joe felt Wishbone press against his leg. Wishbone was craning as if he, too, wanted to get a glimpse of their next-door neighbor. Miss Wanda Gilmore was the president of the Oakdale Historical Society, and Fabulous Fifties Day was largely her project. She was enthusiastic about everything, and Joe could tell from her broad

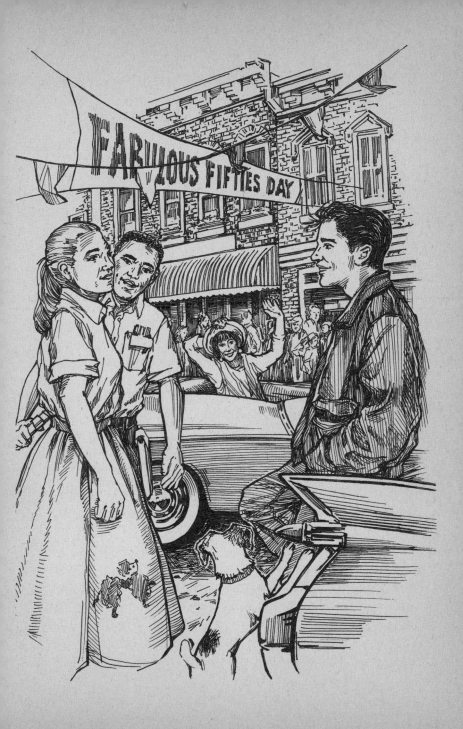

smile and twinkling eyes that she was greatly enjoying her tour of Main Street.

She caught sight of them and called out, "Joe! Sam! David! Come over here! Stop here, Horace."

The friends made their way over to the car. The driver, a heavyset, red-faced man wearing a flat straw hat tilted at a jaunty angle, smiled at them. "Kids," said Wanda, "I want you to meet Mr. Horace Zimmerman, the president of the state's Antique Car Club." She introduced Sam, David, and Joe.

"And who's the short one?" asked Mr. Zimmerman, leaning out to look down at Wishbone.

Wishbone barked.

"He's my dog, sir," Joe said. "His name is Wishbone."

"Look at you," Wanda said. "Great costumes. Kids, remember, this afternoon at one o'clock we're having the big parade of antique cars. Horace, don't you think the kids look wonderful? Couldn't they ride in one of the cars?"

"I think that would be great," Mr. Zimmerman replied. "What about it, Sam, David, Joe? Would you like to ride in one of our restored beauties?"

"Can Wishbone come, too?" Joe asked.

Mr. Zimmerman laughed. "Of course he can, if he's well behaved."

Miss Gilmore stood up in the car, clasping her purple hat to her head and looking around at the crowd. "Oh, dear. We want to start the parade just outside of town, drive up Main Street to the library, back down Main Street, and then out to the Moonlight Drive-In Theater. I need to find Mrs. Glendower, but I don't know where to start—"

"I think she's at the newspaper office," Joe said. "I saw her heading that way a few minutes ago."

"Thanks, Joe," said Wanda. "Oh, this is so thrilling! I'm sure the parade will help her get her drive-in started again. This is a great day for everyone."

"The old drive-in movie theater outside of town?" David asked. "That's been closed for as long as I can remember. Is that going to open again?"

"Maybe," Wanda said. She sighed. "We don't really know. Mrs. Glendower owns it, and she wants to reopen it, but she's having a lot of trouble."

"What kind of trouble?" Joe asked. He didn't know Mrs. Glendower very well, but he saw her around town now and then. She was in her late sixties, and was very active and cheerful.

"Well, different kinds of trouble," Wanda said. "She has to bring the Moonlight up to local health and safety codes, and that's costing a lot of money. And then, too, she says that there's been some trouble out there. Vandalism of some kind."

"That's terrible," Sam said. "She's very sweet. She eats in my dad's pizza parlor every once in a while. Can we help?"

"Maybe," Wanda said brightly. "Help me find her, and we'll ask her—if you all want to help, that is."

Joe looked at the others, and they nodded in agreement. "Sure we do," he said. "It would be great to have a drive-in movie theater nearby. You dig, Sam?"

Sam grinned. "The swellest, Daddy-o!"

David chuckled. "Sounds like we're on the case," he said. "Okay, Miss Gilmore. When you find Mrs. Glendower, tell her our gang is ready to help!"

17

Chapter Two

"Come on, boy!" Joe, looking around for Wishbone, couldn't keep himself from grinning. Fabulous Fifties Day was quite an occasion for Oakdale, and the hot-dog man wasn't the only one who had set up a booth.

Most of the downtown merchants were having a big sidewalk sale, and Joe could see rows of tables all up and down Main Street with bargains galore spread over them. People clustered around them, chattering excitedly, filling the air with a cheerful buzz of conversation about the bargains to be had. But Joe knew that Wishbone wouldn't be distracted by stationery, kitchen utensils, or compact disks of golden oldies.

No, Joe's dog simply had to stop at every booth that sold food. All the high-school clubs and some of the college organizations had set up tables to sell cakes, pies, doughnuts, funnel cakes, cotton candy, and other treats. So Wishbone fell behind his friends every few steps, looking up with bright eyes and twitching his nose at some new delicious aroma.

Joe patted his leg to get Wishbone's attention. "Come *on*, boy!" he said again. "I want to find Mom."

With a long last look at the Arbor Society's pop-corn booth, Wishbone licked his chops, sighed, then came over to join Joe. Main Street was packed, with crowds of people spilling over from the sidewalk right out onto the street. The police had closed the street to parking. There was no danger from the antique Edsels, Studebakers, and other old autos, since they cruised by so slowly.

A happy, rumbly voice stopped Joe in his tracks. "My boy! How are you!"

Joe waved and grinned. Mr. Kilgore Gurney, Oak-dale's favorite used-book dealer, stood behind a row of tables spread with stacks of books written in the fifties. Mr. Gurney was a bespectacled, white-haired, white-bearded Santa Claus of a man, with twinkling eyes and a cheerful laugh. Joe had worked for him at Ren-dezvous Books over the summer. He made his way over, waited while Mr. Gurney completed a sale, then said, "Hi, Mr. Gurney! How's business?"

"Can't complain," Mr. Gurney answered. He waved at a neat, colorful sign, hand-lettered with red, green, and blue markers on a piece of poster board that was hanging from the awning overhead. The sign read: YESTERDAY'S BEST-SELLERS AT YESTERDAY'S PRICES! Mr. Gurney leaned over the tables full of books and said, "And hello to you, too, Wishbone."

Wishbone stretched out his front paws, as if he were bowing to Mr. Gurney.

"Joe, are you in the mood for a fifties book?" Mr. Gurney asked, straightening up and gesturing toward his

tables. "I've got volumes of Sue Barton, the young nurse who had scads of medical adventures! Or if you want to blast into outer space, I've got all the Lucky Starr books by Paul French—better known by his real name, Isaac Asimov—and lots of stuff by Robert Heinlein. I'd recommend *The Star Beast*, one of my favorites. Or maybe you'd like some of the funny Freddy the Pig books by Walter Brooks—they're a little young for you, but only older readers get all the jokes. I know. How about a good dog book by Jim Kjelgaard? *Big Red* is about the *second* smartest dog I know, right after Wishbone!"

"They all sound great, Mr. Gurney," Joe said, "but I just don't have time right now. Have you seen my mom? She's around here somewhere."

Mr. Gurney tugged at his white beard. "Come to think of it, I did, Joe. She was across the street about five minutes ago. I think she was heading toward the library, but very slowly. She was checking out all the booths along the way."

"Thanks!" Joe said. He and Wishbone hurried across Main Street. The other side was just as packed with shoppers. The two pals hurried along the edge of the crowd. Every once in a while, Joe jumped up to see if he could spot his mom over the heads of the people who were examining the booths. Finally, he saw her, standing at a display of stationery and writing supplies.

His mom was a trim, dark-haired woman. She looked up with a smile as Joe and Wishbone worked their way through the crowd. "Having fun?" Ellen asked as they approached.

"Hi, Mom," Joe said. "Wishbone and I got invited to be in the antique-car parade."

"Sounds great," Ellen said. "That ought to be fun for both of you."

"But I thought I should ask you first," Joe explained. "It ends up out at the old drive-in theater, and I wanted to let you know where we would be."

"I suppose you have a way to get back home?"

Joe blinked. He hadn't even thought about asking. "Uh . . . I don't know," he said. "I can find out." He turned, shading his eyes against the sun. "I just have to go ask Miss Gilmore. She's over across the street, next to her T-bird."

"I'll go with you," Ellen said, paying for a pen-and-pencil set. When she had received her change, they all crossed the street again.

The smell of hot dogs was strong, and Joe noticed that Wishbone's tail began to wag hopefully. Wanda was standing beside her cream-colored classic T-bird, talking to David and Sam.

21

"Oh, look at you," Ellen said as they came up to the group. "Sam, you look great!"

Sam blushed and smiled. "My mom and I made the outfit," she said. "Except for the shoes. Dad found those for me."

"Hello, Ellen," Wanda said. She was holding a camera, and she raised it and snapped a quick picture of Ellen, Joe, and Wishbone. "Isn't this just about the greatest thing ever to happen in Oakdale?"

Joe smiled at Sam and David. Wanda tended to believe that everything was just about the greatest thing ever to happen in Oakdale. She was very upbeat, to say the least.

"It was a great idea, Wanda," Ellen agreed. "What's this I hear about the kids being invited to join the parade?"

"Oh, we've been working that out," Wanda said. "Horace Zimmerman is going to drive Joe and Wishbone in his Hudson Hornet. Sam and David are going to ride right behind in Roger Conklin's Mercury convertible. When it's over, I'll bring everyone back home."

Joe could hardly believe his ears. "Mr. Zimmerman has *another* old car?" he asked. "Besides the Chevy, I mean?"

Wanda laughed. "Horace has seventeen or eighteen antique autos," she told Joe. "He's a wealthy man, you know. He owns a chain of restaurants, and cars are his only hobby, so he can afford to indulge himself. He's letting another member of the Antique Car Club drive the Chevrolet. His favorite is the Hudson."

"You don't mind bringing the kids back, Wanda?" asked Ellen.

"Heavens, no!" said Wanda. "I—" Wanda broke off, frowning past Joe.

He turned and looked over his shoulder. Mrs. Glendower stood about thirty feet away, deep in conversation with a stern-looking young man. A girl with curly, light-brown hair stood close to the older woman. She looked worried, and she kept touching Mrs. Glendower's arm reassuringly.

"Poor Mrs. Glendower," muttered Wanda. "I see she's still having trouble with the inspectors."

"What kind of trouble?" Ellen asked.

Wanda shrugged. "Oh, the inspectors have to okay everything before you open a business, you know—or reopen, in this case. The drive-in theater has lots of old wiring that electricians have to update. They have to make sure that those speakers people attach to their cars to hear the movie won't give them an electrical shock, and so on. Then there's the concession building, water and sewer service for the rest rooms, and plenty of other concerns." Wanda lowered her voice. "Between us, I think that the real problem is MegaMall."

Sam looked at Wanda. "I've heard of that," she said. "Isn't that the company that wants to open a big mall in town?"

Joe was surprised. "Where'd you hear that?"

"My dad told me," Sam said. "He's a member of the Chamber of Commerce, remember?"

"Our own mall?" David said. "Wow!" He nudged Joe. "An arcade! A multiplex movie theater! Imagine the possibilities!"

Joe thought the idea sounded great, except for

one thing. He asked Wanda, "How could a mall be a problem for Mrs. Glendower?"

"The corporation would love to buy the land where the Moonlight Drive-In is located to build the mall," said Wanda.

"I see. The theater would be torn down," Joe said. "But wouldn't that be a good business decision for Mrs. Glendower? I mean, if she could get a lot of money for the land?"

"She's not interested in the money," Wanda said. "Gladys just simply wants to reopen the drive-in. Her husband ran it for years, until he passed away. The place means a lot to her."

Ellen nodded. "That drive-in meant a lot to me and other people who grew up here. I can only imagine what it means to Mrs. Glendower."

Glancing back at Mrs. Glendower, who was listening to the stern-looking man and nodding her head slowly, Joe said, "But if Mrs. Glendower wants to sell her land, there's no problem, right?"

"Progress," said Wanda with a sigh. "When new things come along, some old ones have to go." She brightened and looked at her watch. "Well, we don't have to worry about that right now. Mrs. Glendower has a temporary permit to open for this week, and she's planning to show some great movies, for free. Be on time, now. The parade's going to start in fifty-two minutes."

Ellen was the first to leave. David and Sam wanted to do some shopping, but Joe and Wishbone lingered. Joe moved closer to Mrs. Glendower, the teenaged girl, and the young man they were talking to. He overheard the man say, "Yes, I know it's a long list, but all of these items have to be satisfied before you can get a permanent certificate to reopen." He handed her a stapled stack of papers, then turned and walked away.

Joe said quietly, "Hi, Mrs. Glendower."

Mrs. Glendower had braided her gray hair into two pigtails, and she wore a pink blouse with puffy sleeves, white pedal pushers—snug pants with legs that ended halfway down her calves—rolled-down bobby socks, and brown penny loafers. The teenage girl—who Joe guessed was about sixteen—was wearing a similar outfit. They both turned to face Joe.

With some concern, he saw that Mrs. Glendower's eyes were red, as if she had been crying.

She managed a smile and said, "Hello, Joe. Hi, Wishbone. Oh, this is my niece, Kelly Glendower. She's been spending the summer with me."

"Hi," Kelly said, her voice almost a whisper. Her face was freckled and tan, but beneath the tan Kelly was very pink, as if she were upset or embarrassed.

"Hi," Joe said, smiling. Then he turned to Mrs. Glendower. "Are you okay?"

Wishbone sat and looked up, as if expecting a pat on the head, but Mrs. Glendower just sighed. "Yes, I think so. When I first heard about Fabulous Fifties Day, I thought it would be a wonderful time to open the Moonlight again, but it's turning out to be harder than I thought. Every time I think I have all the permits and papers complete, something else comes up."

"Miss Gilmore told us about your problem," Joe said. "If you need help, I'll volunteer. I've got more than a week before school starts again. My friends Sam and David will help, too."

Mrs. Glendower smiled. "That's so kind of you. Yes, I do need help. I have what's called a punch list here—a list of things that I have to do to reopen. Besides that, there's so much painting and repair work."

"I think it's too much for you and your friends to do," said Kelly.

"We can get other kids to pitch in, too," Joe said. "My basketball team can help out, and Sam and David have lots of friends who can lend a hand." He paused. "I heard you had some trouble with vandals," he said.

Mrs. Glendower nodded. "We have, yes. Although the drive-in has been closed ever since my husband died twelve years ago, I've made a point of visiting it every week. I never had any trouble with someone damaging the property until I decided to reopen it." She looked puzzled. "Then a lot of little things started to happen. Someone broke all the outside light bulbs, cut the starter cord for the lawn mower, and punctured a five-gallon paint can and let the paint pour out. Sometimes I feel as if I have an enemy."

"No, Aunt Gladys," Kelly said, patting her arm.

"Now you have some friends," Joe told her. Wishbone chimed in with a bark, as if in agreement. "We'll do everything we can," he promised. *And,* he added mentally, *we'll catch that vandal, too.*

The parade started at one. Wishbone loved riding in cars, and this car was great! He stood on his hind legs and leaned his head out the window, his nose working overtime to bring him the smells of the parade. *I'll bet all the other dogs will think I'm a star,* Wishbone thought proudly. *Not just any mutt gets to be top dog in the big parade!*

Just ahead, Wanda's T-bird rolled grandly along. In the Hudson, Mr. Zimmerman waved from the driver's window to the cheering crowds on either side of the street. Joe sat behind Mr. Zimmerman and tossed candy out to the kids along the route. Wishbone could smell its heavenly peppermint aroma. Wishbone gazed out at the people he passed, and he barked for joy every once in a while.

The parade drove slowly through the business district. From behind the antique cars came the sounds of marching bands from the high school and the college. The closer band, the one from the high school, was playing marching tunes. The college band was playing songs that Wishbone couldn't quite make out, though he could hear the deep boom-boom-boom of the big bass drum.

"Having fun, Wishbone?" Joe asked.

Wishbone gave Joe a happy grin. "You bet, Joe! This is great! I wish dogs could drive. Well, why not? I already have my license!"

Once Mr. Zimmerman got to the outskirts of town, the parade picked up speed. Wishbone saw a couple of orange school buses there. "Those are for the marching bands," Mr. Zimmerman explained over his shoulder. "We're having a picnic out at the drive-in, and this way they won't have to walk for a mile and a half to get there!"

27

Wishbone's ears perked up. "What? Picnic? Picnic? Uh . . . could we go a little faster, Mr. Zimmerman? This dog's got an appetite for outdoor food!"

A little distance away, Mr. Zimmerman made a left turn. They came to a tall sign on their right, with the name of the drive-in on it. On their left was a small building with a ticket window—closed now. A moment later, they drove out onto the asphalt parking lot of the Moonlight Drive-In Theater.

Wishbone could see a huge, fan-shaped parking lot. They were entering at the wide end, which was the rear. Across the lot, at the narrow end, sat a long, low, concrete building. In its roof, soaring high into the sky, was a big white screen, its surface dusty and streaked with dirt and grime. Directly in front of the screen was a grassy playground area, with a sandbox, slides, swings, and a seesaw.

Between the ticket office and the screen there were rows of little slopes. Each slope was marked for parking slots, and Wishbone could see how the slant of the slope allowed cars to park so they would be tilted on an incline facing the screen.

Set into each row, next to where each car would park, were four-foot poles. The poles held speakers so that the people in the cars could hear the movie. Wishbone could see that the asphalt was worn and cracked, with weeds sprouting through in many places.

In the rear of the parking lot, and just across from the ticket booth, was a larger building. Wishbone knew right away this was the concession building. It had a glass front, and a few picnic tables were just outside.

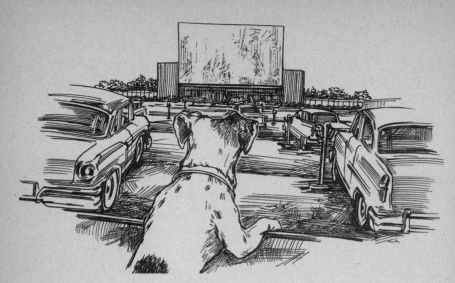

"Ever been out here to the Moonlight before?"
Mr. Zimmerman asked.

"No, sir," Joe said.

Wishbone agreed. "Nope. But this looks like a
civilized kind of drive-in—one where a dog wouldn't
be kept out!"

"That's the concession building, office, and
projection booth," Mr. Zimmerman said, pointing. "I
remember when I was in college, my girlfriend and I
used to enjoy going to the drive-in. You young folks
have been missing out on something special."

Mr. Zimmerman parked the car. A moment later,
the convertible with Sam and David in the backseat
parked next to them. After that, one of the school
buses rumbled in. Joe opened the car door, and Wishbone leaped out, his nose twitching. Across the parking
lot he could see long tables set up. His nose told him
that they held chicken, turkey, roast beef, and other
tasty treats. He started off at a trot.

"Wishbone!"

Wishbone blinked. "But the food's over there, Joe! It's just begging for someone to come along and eat it. That's a tough job, but I'll volunteer!"

"Come back here, Wishbone!"

Reluctantly, Wishbone returned to his friend's side. Other cars were parking now, most of them antique ones. A few newer automobiles came rolling in, and they were followed by the other school bus. Wishbone noticed that some uniformed band members were already lining up at the tables. He sighed.

"Come on," Mr. Zimmerman was saying to Wanda, Joe, David, and Sam. "I'll introduce you to some of the other drivers. You're going to love these machines."

Mrs. Glendower got out of a green Nash Rambler. "Hello again," she said, smiling at Joe. "And hello to you, too, David and Samantha. Joe tells me you'd like to help get the place in shape."

"Sure," David said. "We'll do anything we can to help out."

"Could we look around?" Sam asked.

Wishbone looked up at her pleadingly. "But . . . but . . . I feel the call of roast beef! Turkey! Chicken! Oh, I'm making myself hungry!"

"Well, certainly," Mrs. Glendower said, taking some keys from her purse. "I'll be glad to show you around." She unlocked one of the glass doors of the concession building. "Come right in."

Joe stepped through—and he skidded, his arms flailing. His sunglasses flew off his face, and he barely managed to keep his footing.

Wishbone darted inside, coming to help his friend. "Hang on, Joe—Whoa!" The Jack Russell terrier spun in a complete circle on the slippery black-and-white-checkerboard tile floor. "Help! I'm in a skid!" He came to rest almost halfway across the tile floor, dizzy from the spin.

Joe held on to the door frame. "Don't come in," he warned the others. "It looks like the vandal's struck again!" He lifted his foot from the floor, and gloppy yellow oil dripped from the sole of his biker boot. "Someone's poured oil all over the floor," he said, noticing a few overturned oil containers.

Chapter Three

E veryone clustered at the door, staring at the mess. Joe eased outside. Finally, Wishbone managed to crawl out after him. Joe thought that at least a gallon of the oil had been splashed all over the floor. He sniffed. "There's a strong smell here," he said.

Sam agreed, also sniffing. "That smells like . . . popcorn!"

"That is strange. We haven't made popcorn in here in years. Oh, dear," Mrs. Glendower said. "The kitchen!"

"Is there another way in?" Joe asked.

"Through the office door." Mrs. Glendower led them around the corner. A wooden door opened into a small, square office, where there were a desk, a chair, a sofa, and one small window, which was open.

Joe pointed. "I'll bet that's how the vandal got in," he said.

"I don't see anything disturbed in here," Mrs. Glendower told them. "Let's see what the damage is."

Joe and the others followed Mrs. Glendower through the office to the kitchen, behind the concession counter. More oil was splashed around there.

"This could have caused a serious fire," Mrs. Glendower said. "Look, there is oil on the stove and grill."

Joe could hardly believe the mess in front of them. A couple of gallons of popcorn oil had been splashed everywhere. It gleamed a sickly yellow in the light.

David, who had a very quick grasp of mechanical things, said, "The stove is gas, isn't it?"

"Yes, it is," Mrs. Glendower said.

David looked concerned. "The pilot lights are still on," he said. "Mrs. Glendower, you're lucky the whole place didn't catch fire!"

"I'd better call Mom," Joe said. "This cleaning is going to take longer than I thought."

"The telephone's just behind the counter," Mrs. Glendower told him. "Be careful of where you step."

When Joe turned to go make the call, he saw Wishbone in the office doorway, his nose twitching. "Don't come in," Joe warned him. "You could slip and slide all over the place, and you'd have to have a bath."

Wishbone took one step back, as if agreeing. Joe called home. He explained what happened. Joe reassured his mom there was no further danger of a fire.

Satisfied, she then asked, "What are you going to do for dinner?"

"The Antique Car Club is serving picnic food," Joe told her. "I'll ask Mr. Zimmerman to be sure to save some for us and Wishbone. Mom, we have to help clean up this mess, or the city won't allow Mrs. Glendower to show her movie tonight."

"Do you have plenty of help?" Ellen asked.

"We're fine, Mom," said Joe.

"All right," Ellen said. "You know, I haven't seen a movie in a while. I'll drive out tonight to the Moon-light, and we'll give Sam and David a ride home after the show is over. I'll call their parents and let them know what we're planning."

Joe pitched in with his friends to clean up the oil with what seemed like miles of paper towels and buckets of soapy water. After that, they scrubbed everything down with a strong cleanser and deodorizer. Finally, after several hours, they surveyed their work. The floors gleamed!

"Well," David said, "we're too late for the picnic, but Mr. Zimmerman said he'd save us something. And I want to see all those neat old cars."

As they went outside, Joe could see that twilight was beginning to fall. The sun sank majestically behind the towering screen of the Moonlight Drive-In Theater. More and more antique cars had arrived, lined up in rows by the poles that held the speakers.

"Hi, kids," Horace Zimmerman said as the friends walked tiredly over toward the shiny black Hudson Hornet. "You've really been working hard. Wanda and I saved you all a meal, and there's even a special treat for Wishbone, too."

"Here you are," Wanda said, handing each of them a paper plate piled high with chicken, roast beef, potato salad, and baked beans. She gave Joe a separate plate of ham and roast-beef scraps, too. He placed it on the ground, and Wishbone munched happily.

"Joe," Wanda said, "before you start eating, could

35

you and Mr. Zimmerman get some refreshments at the concession stand?"

"Sure, Miss Gilmore," Joe said.

Wanda was looking through her purse. "Here," she said, holding out a ten-dollar bill. "We ran out of lemonade, so I can't offer you kids anything to drink. Please go to the concession stand and buy soft drinks for everyone. Horace, you go and help him carry them back. Hmm . . . maybe I'd better come along, too."

"I don't know, Wanda," Horace said, running a handkerchief over his damp forehead. "I don't like leaving the Hudson all by itself. . . ."

"Don't be ridiculous, Horace! The Hudson is perfectly capable of entertaining itself! Besides, Sam and David are here. They'll guard it."

"We'll protect it with our lives, Mr. Zimmerman," Sam promised with a smile.

"Well, not with your lives . . ." he said. "All right, let's go."

Wanda smiled. "Thank you, Sam, you're such a dear! Come, Horace, Joe. We've got to get the soft drinks before the pre-movie snack line starts forming! Timing is everything, you know!"

Joe and Wishbone followed Wanda and Mr. Zimmerman up the rise toward the long, low brick building. Wanda's voice floated back at them.

"You're going to love Gladys Glendower, Horace! She is working very hard to get the Moonlight back into shape. That's why the Oakdale Historical Society is so interested in her work. Do you know there are only a few hundred drive-ins left in the entire United States? Once there were more than four thousand of them, one in almost every little town." Wanda paused and gestured widely. "Just look at the sweep of that concession building! Isn't that the most perfect example of classic fifties architecture you ever saw? Why, the colors alone . . ."

"Yes, Wanda."

"Boy, Wishbone," Joe whispered under his breath, looking toward the building. "It may be historical, but from here it sure looks shabby."

It was true. The bricks had splotches of green moss clinging to them. The pink trim was chipped and cracked. Joe remembered that inside the building, the pink and cream colors had been redone in spots, so that it looked as if the walls had a rash.

Wanda and Horace went in to the concession building, and Wishbone started to sniff the ground. Joe thought Wishbone had some business to conduct, so he waited just outside the door. Then he heard voices coming from behind the building. Curious, Joe wandered back to see who was there.

In the harsh white light of an overhead lamp, a long modern black limousine sat parked across three parking spaces, its engine throbbing like the purring of an elegant metal cat. On the side, a small white sign displayed the words "MegaMall Inc." in distinct red letters. Two women and a man stood under the light. Joe recognized only one of them, Mrs. Glendower.

Gladys Glendower was standing with her back toward him, but Joe could still see her wringing her hands. She was talking to a tall, lean man with a hawk nose, brown hair, and dark eyes. "I know I promised to think about it, Mr. Bliss," she said, her voice strained. "But I really don't—"

Wishbone came around the corner and stopped by Joe.

"Our offer is a good fifteen percent over the fair market value for the property, Mrs. Glendower," the lean man interrupted smoothly. His mouth smiled, but the friendly expression didn't quite reach his eyes.

"Oh, it's a very generous offer, Mr. Bliss," Gladys Glendower agreed. "But I've owned the Moonlight for years, and I've already done some work to get it back into shape."

"And, of course, we will want to compensate you for any sentimental value." The lean man nodded to the attractive blond woman in a business suit standing next to him. She nodded back and turned to Gladys, who took a small step backward.

"Mr. Bliss is prepared to offer an additional ten percent to our current offer, Mrs. Glendower, for emotional distress." The woman did some rapid figuring on a hand-held calculator. "That would bring Mega-Mall's final offer to . . ." She held the screen up to Gladys. Joe couldn't see the final figure, but it must have been high. The older woman's jaw dropped.

"That . . . that's an awful lot of . . ."

"Yoo-hoo, Joe!" Wanda Gilmore called out gaily, walking toward Joe. She had come from inside the concession building. "Where did you disappear to? We need you to help carry the soft drinks!"

The woman in the business suit looked up, startled. The lean man's cold black eyes zeroed in on Joe and Wanda like the cannons in a battleship turret. Joe gulped. Even Wishbone seemed to be nervous. Then the man's cold, unfriendly smile slipped right back into place.

He swung his gun-sight eyes back on Gladys. "But you have guests. This is an important night for you, and we've taken up enough of your time," he purred, his voice a cultured rumble, like the engine of his long black car. "You have my offer, Mrs. Glendower. We will continue our conversation later."

"Yes, Mr. Bliss, later . . . that would be . . . nice."

Whoa! Scary guy! Wishbone thought as the man nodded at Gladys, then opened the limousine door. The woman in the business suit paused by the open door, looked around, then got into the car. *She's scary, too!* Her employer closed the door and went to the other side and opened that door. Wishbone let out a low growl.

As faint as the growl was, the man heard it and stopped. His black eyes lowered until he was staring right at Wishbone, who had moved between him and Joe. Wishbone stared hard at the man. "Hold it right there, Scary Guy! Don't mess with a dog's best friend!"

"Ah," the lean man said lightly. "And what do we have here? A Jack Russell terrier, unless I miss my guess." The black eyes swiveled up to Joe.

"Yes, sir. His name is Wishbone."

Wishbone glanced up sharply at his buddy. "Don't tell him anything, Joe! He reminds me of a German shepherd I used to know. They didn't call him Ripper because he liked to open envelopes!"

"I thought so. A very intelligent breed of dog, Ms. Corwin."

From the open window of the limousine, the attractive woman looked at Wishbone critically. "If you say so, Mr. Bliss."

Wishbone sniffed pointedly. The man's cold smile cut farther across his face. "Oh, I do, Ms. Corwin, I do." Then he got into the car. A moment later, the tinted, electric window was closed, and the big limo rolled slowly away.

Wishbone stared after them. "There's something about those two that makes my fur stand on end—and if a dog can't trust his own fur, what can he trust?"

Joe noticed that everyone was very quiet until they all heard the big limousine prowl away into the night. Then there was a collective sigh of relief.

"Who was that strange man?" Wanda asked Gladys, who was leaning up against the concession-building wall as if she might fall down any minute.

"That was Mr. Harry Bliss of MegaMall Inc., and his assistant, Ms. Corwin." Gladys tried to put on a smile, although it was a shaky one. "I'm so glad you came along, Wanda. For some reason, I'm a little afraid of him. I guess it's silly of me."

Joe was holding Wishbone and staring out into the now empty twilight. "I don't think it's silly," he said. "He doesn't seem like a very friendly man." Wishbone seemed to nod in agreement.

"Bliss . . . Bliss," Horace muttered. Then he

snapped his fingers. "MegaMall! I read about him in one of my business magazines. He's a big real estate and construction tycoon—rich as they come. What's a man like that doing here in Oakdale?"

"He wants to buy the Moonlight so he can tear it down and build a huge regional shopping mall here," Mrs. Glendower said with a sigh.

Wanda sniffed. "Well, I'm certain you told him that was out of the question!"

"He's offering a lot of money, Wanda," Mrs. Glendower said.

"Tear down the Moonlight! Gladys Glendower, you're opening the Moonlight for sentimental reasons, remember? Don't do something you'll regret—unless money is more important."

They all walked over to the concession stand, where Joe saw a couple of trays filled with soft drinks waiting on the counter.

Mrs. Glendower sighed. "Well, I don't want to sell, but the renovation costs keep growing higher and higher. Then, on top of that, we have strange accidents, like the one Joe and his friends helped me clean up this afternoon. . . ."

Gladys's hands fluttered back and forth as if they were suddenly going to turn into pigeons and fly right off her wrists.

"But I guess I'll work it out somehow. You know, old Ralph Turpin volunteered to be the projectionist without taking any salary. He ran the Moonlight's projector for thirty years, and he says that being retired is boring. With help like that, I might just make it."

"Of course you will!" Wanda snapped decisively.

"Because the Oakdale Historical Society is going to help you! We'll have a Fix-Up Project for you! I'll place a front-page notice announcing the event in the *Chronicle* right away."

Mrs. Glendower smiled weakly. "That's nice, but it's so much work—"

Joe smiled. He knew that when Wanda set her mind on doing something, there were no "buts" about the question. Wanda would organize her Fix-Up Project— no matter what happened.

Sure enough, Wanda cut off Mrs. Glendower's faint objection. "Don't you worry about a thing, Gladys! Horace!" Mr. Zimmerman jumped. "What would be a good day to start?"

"Well, Monday is pretty . . ."

"Monday! What a perfect idea! Would Monday be good for you, Gladys?"

Joe thought that Mrs. Glendower looked a little stunned as she said, "Well, I don't see why not . . ."

"Perfect! I'll get to work on it immediately! Horace, you and Joe carry the soft drinks. You do know Horace, don't you, Gladys? . . . No? Oh. Gladys Glendower, this is Horace Zimmerman, of the Antique Car Club. Horace, this is Gladys. Now that we have the formal intro-ductions out of the way, there's so much to do! I have to make phone calls and arrange to put a big notice in the paper and—"

Mrs. Glendower seemed totally lost. She whispered to Horace, "She's a bit overwhelming, isn't she?"

"Don't worry, Mrs. Glendower," Horace said kindly. "Everyone feels that way about Wanda. It's part of her charm."

"Picnic time!" Wishbone bounded across the parking lot, his head stuffed with visions of food. "It's picnic time! Maybe a couple more plates of scraps, then maybe some buttered popcorn for the movie, and then maybe some—"

Joe and Horace followed, each carrying a small tray of soft drinks. Ellen drove up just as they got to the Hudson, and Horace put together second helpings for everyone—including Wishbone. Then he offered a plate of cold chicken and potato salad to Ellen.

"Thanks," Ellen said with a smile, "but I've already had dinner. I'd like a soft drink, though. Where's Wanda?"

Handing her a cup, Horace said, "Oh, she's planning a special Fix-Up Project to help out Mrs. Glendower. She stayed back at the concession stand to work out a schedule."

Sam and David grinned at Joe as he handed them their soft drinks. "Looks like we're going to be volunteered for some more drive-in movie duty," David said cheerfully. "I sort of wondered if just cleaning up the oil would be the end of it. Guess not! Joe, Sam, we'd better call around tomorrow for reinforcements. It's going to take a lot of effort to get this place in shape."

Ellen said, "I'd like to help, but I can't—not next week. I'm going to be too busy with the annual library inventory."

Joe said, "That's okay, Mom. We can handle it."

He was happy that both his friends didn't seem to

mind joining in the renovation effort. Not that it made much difference—when Wanda was enthusiastic about a cause, everyone just sort of felt swept along.

Joe happily munched his dinner. When Wishbone sat at his feet giving him the Big Puppy Eyes look, he had to laugh. He pulled some meat off the drumstick—he knew that chicken bones could choke a dog—and tossed it to Wishbone, who promptly gobbled it down and waited for more to come his way.

"I can see how we're supposed to see the movie," David said around a drumstick, nodding toward the giant screen. "But how are we supposed to *hear* it?"

"With the speakers, of course," Horace said, sounding surprised. He walked toward the metal pole in the asphalt next to his car. A square, slotted box hung on the pole, connected to it by a long wire. He took it off and hooked it on the driver's-side window, with the speaker pointing inside.

David squinted at it. "The sound comes from that one little speaker?"

With a laugh, Mr. Zimmerman said, "It's not a fifteen-channel stereo or anything fancy, but it gets the job done. Most of the surviving drive-ins have low-power radio transmitters, so you listen to the sound over your car radio. I like these old single speakers, though. Now, you can adjust the sound with this little knob right here. . . . Wow!"

The square box burst into a blast of static as the huge screen exploded into light. Then the light dissolved into bright, dancing, animated letters that spelled out *Coming Attractions.*

"In the groove, Daddy-o, in the groove!" Sam sang out, laughing.

"In the groove?" Joe asked, looking at his mother.

Ellen looked back at him and shrugged. "You're just not hep, Joe."

Later, as they watched the movie, Joe began to understand the special appeal of drive-ins. The warm summer air, the large, bright screen (even if it was streaked in places with dust and grime), and the dark, star-sprinkled sky all made the experience very different from watching an indoor movie or television. It was almost magical. In the car they could talk without disturbing anyone else. Now and then a high-flying plane would appear in the distance in the sky above the screen, its blinking red and green lights moving lazily across the background of night.

Best of all, the first movie of the double feature was the classic horror film *House of Wax.* Joe, David, Sam, and Ellen all put on special cardboard glasses, with one red and one blue lens. The movie was in 3-D. When a ball came toward the camera, Joe, Sam, and David all ducked, because it looked as if it were coming straight at them! They got a real thrill with that. Then, in an exciting, scary scene in which a wax museum burned, they jumped when the wooden beams crashed down, and the ghastly melting heads of the wax dummies turned into molten liquid. Even then they laughed together at their own startled reactions.

Wishbone, Joe thought, was enjoying the show. Wishbone had decided to sit outside the car. He was right up front, on the grassy playground in front of the screen, his head tilted back. When the movie ended and a cartoon came on in which a cat and mouse fought each other, Wishbone's tail began to thump.

Joe pointed that out to Ellen. "I think he's rooting for the mouse," Joe told her, as he watched a cat get an anvil, a safe, a house, an ocean liner, and the Empire State Building dropped on him from outer space.

When the second movie of the double feature came on, Wishbone couldn't take his eyes off the screen. Well, Joe decided, why not? The movie featured one of the most famous screen dogs of all time, Lassie.

When he noticed how much everyone enjoyed the movie, Joe's determination rose. He and his friends were not only going to help Mrs. Glendower get the old drive-in cleaned up—they were also going to catch the sneaky vandal who was trying to destroy it.

Chapter Four

Beep! Beep-beep! The sound of the car horn jolted Wishbone right out of a deep sleep. "I'm up! I'm up! Hey, Joe! Emergency wake-up call here!"

Joe sat up in bed, yawning. "Who's making all that noise?" he wondered out loud. He looked at his alarm clock. "Six-thirty! It's still practically dark outside," Joe mumbled to Wishbone as he started to dress. "Who gets up at six-thirty on a summer morning?"

"I know one way to find out, Joe—let's take a look!" Wishbone waited at the door, circling impatiently. Joe tugged his sneakers on, tied them, and then the two of them went downstairs to see what the noise was all about.

Ellen, still in her robe, was just opening the front door. "Wanda!" Ellen called out at her neighbor in surprise. "Was that you?"

"Yes!" Wanda said briskly, as she carried a box to her car. Wishbone could see that she was dressed in gray overalls and a painter's cap. "It's Moonlight Drive-

In's first Fix-Up day! Have breakfast, put on your working clothes, and come on out as soon as possible!"

"I thought it started later," Ellen said, looking at her watch. "Like about nine or so."

"The early bird gets the worm, Ellen!" Wanda said cheerfully.

Wishbone blinked. "Sure, but who wants a sleepy worm, Wanda?"

Wanda was looking past Ellen, talking to Joe. "Hurry on out now, just as soon as you can! Oh, Ellen, would you mind picking up David and Sam? They're coming to help, too, and I want to get out to the drive-in early. I suppose the other young people will arrange their own rides."

"Sure," Ellen said. "Maybe I won't blow my horn for Sam and David, though. It's pretty early to be making that kind of noise. And I'll have to drop them off and run, because I'm due at the library by nine-thirty."

"Boy," Joe said as Wanda's T-bird pulled away from the curb. "When Miss Gilmore has a pet project, nobody sleeps!"

Ellen smiled and shook her head. "Well, Wanda can be very enthusiastic. How about cereal and fruit for breakfast?"

"Sounds good," Joe said.

He got Wishbone's breakfast ready while Ellen was busy setting the table and getting out the corn flakes, strawberries, and milk. Wishbone gobbled his dry food with great appreciation, and he was finished before Ellen had sat down at the table.

Joe kept yawning and shaking his head. As he munched his cereal, he said, "I started to read one of

Dad's old books last night. It's got a really weird title, but it sort of reminds me of what's happening at the drive-in."

"What's the title?" Ellen asked.

Joe grinned. "It's called *The Roman Hat Mystery.* It's a detective story by someone named Ellery Queen. Have you ever heard of it?"

Wishbone had been chasing down one last particle of dry food. His head snapped up at once. "Ellery Queen! A master of mystery! A great storyteller! In fact, he was so great that just one person couldn't be Ellery Queen—there were two!"

Ellen put on her librarian expression of concentration. "I read the book, but it was quite a few years ago. I am familiar with the author. Let me see . . . if I remember right, 'Ellery Queen' was a pseudonym, or pen name, of two cousins who wrote mysteries together. I believe their real names were Manfred Lee and Frederick Dannay. Their first mysteries all had some nationality in the title—*The Roman Hat Mystery, The French Powder Mystery, The Spanish Cape Mystery, The Chinese Orange Mystery*, and so on. How am I doing?"

Wishbone laid his head on his paws. "Oh, you're doing great. I just wish that sometimes someone would listen to the dog!"

Joe laughed. "Right," he said. "You're a great reference librarian, Mom. Well, *The Roman Hat Mystery* was the very first Ellery Queen book. Did you know that Ellery Queen was a character in the books, and not just the pen name of the writers?"

Wishbone jumped up again. "I knew that!" He looked proudly at Ellen.

Ellen smiled at her son and said, "I had some idea of that, yes."

Wishbone grinned. "Me, too, Ellen."

Joe said, "In this book, there's a New York theater called the Roman Theater, and a strange murder takes place there. A greedy, sort-of-nosy businessman named Monte Field is poisoned while watching a play. No one knows how the murder could have been done. It's almost as if there's a phantom who can slip in and out of the theater without being seen—just the way someone dumped all that popcorn oil at the concession building without being caught."

"Have you finished the book yet?"

Joe shook his head. "No. It's interesting, though, because Ellery Queen doesn't look for just physical clues, like fingerprints. He says that psychological clues—the way people think and behave—are just as important."

Wishbone barked.

Ellen got up from the table, smiling. "I think Wishbone's psychology tells him he wants seconds for breakfast," she said, getting a box of dog food from the kitchen shelf.

Wishbone stood by his bowl, his tail wagging. "Thanks for listening to the dog, Ellen. You're all right where it counts. And that's in the food department!" He started to eat his second serving as if he'd never had a first one.

Ellen put the food box back on the shelf. "Joe, I'll shower and get ready. Maybe you can call Sam and David. I hope their parents don't mind your calling them so early."

A still-sleepy Joe made both phone calls. Luckily, both times his friends answered the phone. David mumbled and Joe had to repeat himself several times—Joe's call had awakened him—but Sam was already up and ready to go. After he had made the arrangements, Joe ran upstairs, brushed his teeth, and came back downstairs to find Ellen was already there, dressed in jeans and a sweatshirt, waiting beside the door. Wishbone had gone outside after breakfast and came back in through his doggie door. "Can Wishbone come, too?" Joe asked.

"I don't think that's a problem," Ellen said. "There's plenty of room for him to run around. And who knows? Wanda just may put him to work!"

Joe went next door to pick up David. Wishbone sat on Joe's lap as they drove over and picked up Sam. Wishbone abandoned Joe as soon as Sam climbed into the backseat. He seemed to like the way Sam fussed over him and scratched his ears. He settled down between Sam and David in the back, with what looked to Joe like a happy grin on his face.

Joe looked out the window as his mom drove through Oakdale and then to the outskirts of town. He blinked in the early morning light. Up ahead, pickup trucks, cars, and vans were turning in at the Moonlight Drive-In Theater's entrance. "It looks as if Wanda has really been busy!" he said.

Ellen turned in at the driveway, too, and they rolled slowly past the ticket booth. Some of the guys from Joe's intramural basketball team were inside, dressed in white coveralls. They busily used rollers to give the inside of the booth a fresh coat of shiny, apple-green paint.

Two dozen cars, trucks, and vans were already parked in the lot, and many kids were already hard at work. A crew of six men was assembling a metal scaffold in front of the big screen. A girl from school was up on a tall ladder, painting the trim around the roof of the concession building. The smell of the paint drifted sharp and clear on the morning air.

"I'll see the three of you—and you, too, Wishbone—later," said Ellen.

"There's Miss Gilmore," Sam said, as she climbed out of Ellen's Explorer.

Joe looked in the direction that she was pointing. Wanda stood next to Gladys Glendower, and they were talking to a short man in a dark suit. The man was very thin, bald on top, and he carried a clipboard.

Joe said, "Come on," and led the way over.

". . . I'm really sorry," Joe heard the short man say. "I hate to be discouraging, but the wiring in the kitchen will have to be replaced. There's also a fire regulation that says all theaters must have at least four clearly marked exits—"

"That's only for indoor theaters! This is a drive-in!" exclaimed Wanda.

"But the fire code doesn't state anything about a theater being an indoor or an outdoor theater," replied the man in a tone that sounded a little desperate, Joe thought. "It just says theaters, period."

"Hi," Joe said, coming up behind Wanda.

"Oh, hello, Joe," she said. "I was just telling Mr. Penny, here, that he has nothing to worry about. The Oakdale Historical Society will bring the Moonlight up to code in no time."

"Uh . . . *up to code?*" he asked as Sam, David, and Ellen caught up to him.

Mr. Penny, whose eyes were mild and blue behind round spectacles, nodded. "That's right. You see, there are strict codes that govern all public buildings. Places like this have to have safe electrical wiring, sanitary plumbing, accessible fire exits, and other things. And if they serve food, they have to prove that their food-preparation areas are clean and hygienic, and they have to have licenses—"

"It's all a lot more complicated than it used to be when my husband ran the Moonlight," Mrs. Glendower said, a bit overwhelmed. "My stars, if I'd realized how much trouble it would all cause, I would certainly have thought twice about trying to reopen the old place."

Wishbone sniffed Mr. Penny's shoes, and the man nervously edged away from him. "Is that your dog?" Mr. Penny asked.

Joe said quickly, "He's had all his shots, and he has his dog license. And he doesn't bite. Come here, Wishbone!"

"Thank you," Mr. Penny said.

Wishbone gave the brown shoes one last sniff, then trotted back to Joe. He sat down and looked up expectantly. "Good boy," Joe told him.

"He won't be allowed in the food-preparation area, will he?" asked Mr. Penny. "Because that would be a violation of an ordinance, and I'd have to write you up for that."

Joe began to understand Wanda's grim expression. "No, sir," he said quickly. "I'll keep him outside."

Mr. Penny nodded absently, then looked at the papers on his clipboard. "Well, as I say, Mrs. Glendower, you've got a lot to do before you can bring this old place up to code—quite a lot to do. And, of course, the interior rewiring must be done by licensed electricians. Then the fire marshall will have to make his inspection. I hope you can make it."

"We'll make it together," Wanda announced firmly. "Never fear."

They walked over to the concession building. Wishbone looked up hopefully. "I'll be glad to pitch in and help, gang! Now, if Mrs. Glendower has any food she wants to dispose of, I've got some great ideas about who can do it!"

"What do you want us to do?" Joe asked Mrs. Glendower.

The drive-in owner did not have a chance to reply. Wanda said, "I've been thinking about that. Of course, you aren't licensed electricians or anything, but I think you can all hold brushes or paint rollers with the best of them, so I want you to paint the screen. We've got safety harnesses and everything else you need. I've checked with your parents and reassured them of your safety. But first I want to show you a book about drive-ins and run some of my redecorating ideas by you. Come along! We have a lot of work to do." They reached the building.

Wishbone came right up to the door, following everyone else. Then he stopped when Joe turned around and said, "You're not supposed to come in here, boy. Sorry."

Wishbone cocked his head. "What! Surely there's no city ordinance against handsome, intelligent dogs supervising painters! I protest!"

"It's all right, Joe," Wanda said, "as long as he doesn't go into the back, in the kitchen."

Wishbone let his ears droop a little. "How unfair can you get! My favorite place, and I'm banned!"

But he came inside, and he watched from a sunny corner of the floor while Wanda flopped a huge, oversized book on the counter. "Now, here are my ideas," she said. "Gather around, Joe, David, and Sam. This is a book about the architecture of the country's greatest drive-in theaters. Here's a page on one that we could use as a model for redecorating the Moonlight. . . ."

Wishbone yawned as his friends examined the book. Then he amused himself by playing "guess the aroma." His sensitive nose really strained to bring him news of all the types of food that had been served here over the years. "Hmm . . . there's pizza, with pepperoni, mushrooms, hamburger, and—once someone ordered anchovies." He sniffed deeply. "Just once. About fifteen years ago, if I'm not mistaken. And there's popcorn, of course. Candy of all kinds. Chocolate, peppermint, even—yuck!—licorice. Hot dogs." He sniffed again. "Hamburgers. A sheep dog. Potato chips— Wait a minute!"

Wishbone leaped to his feet.

"Sheep dog?"

He padded over to the door that led outside, his nose working overtime. Through the glass he saw a huge, shaggy form. Kelly Glendower, Mrs. Glendower's niece, opened the door and walked inside. Suddenly the big dog was right in front of Wishbone, leaning over to sniff curiously. Their noses almost touched.

Wishbone had to blink his eyes. He couldn't tell if the sheepdog blinked or not—Wishbone couldn't even *see* his eyes! But the other dog was wagging his tail in a friendly way, and so Wishbone did, too. "Hi! Pleased to sniff you!"

"Joe, you'd better move poor little Wishbone if you don't want Shemp to step on him accidentally!" Kelly said, trying to hold the excited dog back.

Wishbone gave her a dignified look. *"Little?* Excuse me, but there are no little dogs around here that I can see!"

"Here, Wishbone!" called Joe. Wishbone obediently went over and sat next to Joe's feet. "So that's Shep, is it?"

"Not Shep," Kelly corrected. "Shemp. S-h-e-m-p. He's named after one of the Three Stooges." To Mrs. Glendower, she said, "Aunt Gladys, I called the gas company. They'll send someone over to check out the stove today."

"Thank you, dear," said Mrs. Glendower. "Oh, I'm forgetting my manners. Everyone, this is my niece, Kelly. She's been spending the summer with me, helping me plan for the big reopening. Kelly, this is Miss Gilmore, Sam, and David. You've already met Joe. They're helping fix up the drive-in so we can reopen for business."

"Good luck," Kelly said.

Wishbone looked up at Kelly. *Strange. She doesn't seem very enthusiastic about the project.*

Shemp turned around and scratched at the door. "You can let him out," Mrs. Glendower said. "He won't get into any trouble."

Wishbone jumped up, also. "I'd like to go out now, too, please!"

"Can Wishbone go, too?" Joe asked. "He usually gets along great with other dogs."

"Of course," Mrs. Glendower said. "We'll check on them every once in a while, but I'm sure they'll be perfectly fine."

Wanda was rummaging through a box. "Here you

are," she said, producing three baggy sets of coveralls that might have been white once, before many, many years of paint spatters. "Everyone suit up, and then grab a brush!"

Wishbone trotted to the door. "Hate to leave you when you're having so much fun. But I can't hold a brush, and the only way I could paint would be to dip my tail into the can and wag the color on! Later, guys!"

Chapter Five

The morning sun was high, spilling warm yellow light over the Moonlight Drive-In parking lot. Feeling a little clumsy, Joe fumbled at the buttons of the paint-spattered coveralls Wanda had provided. Sam and David were shaking out their own pairs.

"Anyone want to trade?" Sam asked, holding the baggy garment up against her body. The sleeves dangled about six inches past her fingers. "I take something a little more petite, myself."

David chuckled, holding up his coveralls. "I think I must have your size, Sam. I was wondering how I would squeeze into these."

They exchanged coveralls, and Joe, already in his own outfit, watched them awkwardly pull their work clothes on. He moved his arms, feeling the paint-stiffened sleeves crackle almost like paper. "This is going to be different," he said, looking across the asphalt lot at the big screen. The scaffolding was in place. High above the ground, three painters were already at work with long-handled rollers, putting a new coat of white paint on the old screen.

David looked around. "Okay, we're properly clothed and volunteered. Now what next? Where do we start?"

"I guess we go over to the scaffolding and grab some rollers," Joe replied, opening the door and shading his eyes with his hands. The morning light was so bright that he had to squint, his eyes watering a little.

The three friends started to walk across the lot. More and more cars were pouring into the Moonlight's lot. Most were just everyday minivans and station wagons and sedans, but some were the restored and pampered machines of the Antique Car Club.

Joe whistled softly under his breath. "Look at that gray-and-burgundy car. That's an Auburn! And check out that pink Cadillac with the giant tail fins. Wow! That thing's almost big enough to live in!" Joe had learned a lot about antique cars from his dad, before he died of a rare blood disorder when Joe was six. Now, seeing a classic car reminded Joe of his dad.

"What I don't understand are the tail fins," David said with a frown. "I mean, are they supposed to be aerodynamic?"

"What they are supposed to be is *tail fins!*" called a jolly voice. The kids turned and waved as Horace Zimmerman drove up in his Hudson.

"Hi, Mr. Zimmerman," Joe called as the car stopped next to them. "Does Miss Gilmore have you running errands?"

"You might say that." Horace laughed, getting out

of the Hudson and carefully closing the door. "This is my third trip today. You kids ready for work?"

Joe looked at his two friends and nodded. "We're ready."

"Better get to it, then. And be careful!"

Joe, Sam, and David climbed up a ladder onto the scaffolding. The height made Joe a little queasy.

A short, wiry old man, also painting—he introduced himself as Ralph Turpin, the volunteer projectionist—showed them how to get into their safety harnesses. "Just concentrate on the painting," he advised, "and you won't get dizzy."

The other kids on the platform below them called out greetings as Joe and his friends began to use rollers with long extension poles to paint a new layer on the big screen.

"Is this special movie-screen paint?" David asked. "Does it reflect light better than other paint does?"

Mr. Turpin smiled and shook his head. "Nope. Just plain old white oil-based paint. If you want to look for special stuff, you'd have to look elsewhere in the Moonlight."

Joe wondered what he meant. "What kind of special stuff?"

"Well," Mr. Turpin said, his lean muscles moving as he rolled paint onto the screen, "the projectors are special, for instance. Got two of 'em. Modern theaters don't, you know—they just use one, and what's called a platter to hold the whole movie. At the Moonlight, though, I have to have one projector loaded with a reel while the other one is running. Then, when the first projector is about to run out of film, at just the right moment I turn on the second projector. The timing has to be absolutely perfect. That's an art. That's kind of special."

"I'm surprised the projectors still work," David said, panting a little. The long rollers were heavy.

Mr. Turpin laughed. "No mystery there. I've been tinkering with 'em for a couple of months. They're in fine shape. I just hope we don't blow any bulbs, which we call lamps, before the drive-in starts to bring in some money. They cost about two thousand dollars apiece to replace!"

Joe whistled. That was pretty expensive.

The morning grew warmer, and the team of seven made progress. Mr. Turpin's phrase "no mystery there" had reminded Joe of the Ellery Queen book he was reading. He told David and Sam about *The Roman Hat Mystery*. "Ellery Queen's a real genius," he added. "He notices every little thing—"

David laughed. "I've just noticed that you've missed a spot, Joe. Hey, don't tell us the ending. You're making me want to read the book."

"Okay," agreed Joe. But he continued telling David and Sam about some of the very clever things Ellery Queen had done in the story. By eleven o'clock, they had repainted the top third of the screen and had descended to the next level of the scaffold. They were still pretty high up. Joe leaned on the railing as they rested for a few moments and gazed out over the drive-in lot. He was surprised at the amount of trash he saw, and he mentioned that to Mr. Turpin.

Mr. Turpin shook his head. "One of the drawbacks of a drive-in," he said. "Folks finish eating and sometimes dump their leftovers out the car windows. It's a clean-up problem every morning after a show."

"Well," Sam said with a smile, "at least we're not on the clean-up crew!"

The great Fix-Up Project rolled on into full swing. As the kids painted their way down the screen, more and more people arrived to pitch in. Joe caught sight of Mr. Zimmerman several times, running back and forth for cleaning supplies and paint. A huge old truck drove up with a fresh supply of lumber tied to its ancient trailer.

And through it all dashed Wanda Gilmore in an old golf cart stacked with reference books and research papers and sheet after sheet of color swatches. In one of her trips past the screen, she excitedly called up to the kids that the golf cart was one of the car club's antique vehicles. It had originally belonged to a movie comedian named W. C. Fields, and it was quite valuable.

Then she zoomed off to where a team of men from Oakdale Roofing were putting new tiles on the ticket booth. She nearly took out a row of speaker posts as she drove over.

Wanda's sure having a lot of fun, Joe thought as he dipped his roller in a tray of paint. *I wonder where Mrs. Glendower is—we haven't seen her or her niece since we first got here. And where is Wishbone?*

Wishbone yipped excitedly as he bounded along the grassy area bordering on the parking lot. "Over here, Shemp! It's another hot dog! Whoa! Maybe even two hot dogs!" He paused to sniff the air expertly. "Wait a minute, I've got this, don't tell me, don't tell me . . . two hot dogs—one with mustard, one with ketchup and onions. . . . Oh, yeah!"

And he was off and running again. The giant shaggy form of Shemp the sheepdog lumbered after him, barking as he struggled to keep up.

Wishbone had decided he liked Shemp. He was, after all, another dog, and dogs should try to stick together. Wishbone tracked the delicious scent to two small pieces of bun and hot dog that someone had tossed out of a car window Saturday night. "Aha! Hot dogs! What did I tell you? Does the nose know, or does the nose know?"

Shemp shambled to a stop and wolfed down the tidbit with the ketchup—and the onions.

Wishbone shuddered. "Ah, that's okay, I'll just take the one with the mustard—you actually ate those onions, didn't you? And you're smiling? It's hard to tell with you."

The two dogs had roamed back and forth across the asphalt lot, doing their part by cleaning up as much discarded edible food as they could find. Their major discovery had been two perfectly good hamburgers that someone had dropped accidentally.

Humans are so strange, Wishbone thought as he remembered the burgers. *Don't they know that dropping food on the ground improves the flavor? Kitchen floors are the best, but a parking lot will do in a pinch.*

In fact, the morning would have been absolutely wonderful if it hadn't been for the long black limo. Several times Wishbone had looked up from tracking down nachos and pizza crusts just in time to catch sight of the evil-looking automobile as it had cruised silently down the road in front of the drive-in. It had never stopped, had never really even slowed down, but it had passed by at least three times.

Wishbone knew in his canine heart that if the limo was there, then scary Harry Bliss must be seated in the back, smiling his cold smile. Wishbone shuddered, as if a gust of wind had suddenly blown across the lot; a cold, wet autumn wind. "Harry Bliss. Now, there's a sinister guy!"

Shemp paused from gobbling down a bit of fried chicken to snort, as if in agreement.

Wishbone looked around. "Gotta keep an eye out so I can warn Joe if they do anything . . . uh . . . scary." Wishbone's nose twitched. He licked his chops. "Whoa! Someone dropped an oatmeal cookie!"

But even as Wishbone made a rush toward the pile of broken crumbs—to keep them from escaping, naturally—he continued to think about Harry Bliss, and just the creepy guy's name made the fur stand up along his back.

Scary guy!

"Hi, Mom! I'm home!" Joe called. He collapsed into a kitchem chair, sighing in relief. It felt wonderful to stretch his legs out. "I'm tired!"

"Glad you're home," his mother replied from upstairs. Wishbone flopped down next to Joe.

Joe reached down and ruffled his pal's ears, and Wishbone licked his fingers. "Wishbone's tired, too."

Ellen came down and stood in the doorway. "You do look as if you've worked hard. I'm sure Mrs. Glendower *and* Wanda are pleased."

Joe stretched until he could almost hear his spine creak. "We painted the *entire* screen! It was kind of neat at the end to look up at all that white paint and know that we did it ourselves." He glanced down at the motionless Wishbone and grinned. "If I'd eaten all the junk you and that shaggy old sheepdog scarfed up, I'd be tired, too." Wishbone opened one eye. Joe laughed and said, "I just want to take a shower, have dinner, and crawl into bed."

Ellen said, "You've been working all day in the sun. A shower would be a great idea." Then she paused and pointedly sniffed the air. "Right now would be a good time."

"Sure thing, Mom." Joe laughed, then groaned as he levered himself up out of the chair. "What are we having for dinner?"

"Probably hot dogs and hamburgers and nachos and popcorn—I think there's probably going to be a lot of popcorn."

Joe didn't understand that at all. "Huh? We're having popcorn for dinner?"

"No, Joe." His mother laughed. "We're having popcorn *after* dinner. I just got off the phone from speaking to Wanda. The first day of her Fix-Up Project went so well that Gladys wants to show her appreciation to everyone. So tonight she's hosting another special showing at the Moonlight—for everyone who helped out today."

"We're going back to the drive-in? Tonight?"

"A free movie, all the food you can eat, *and* no painting. Okay?" Ellen asked. Joe nodded. "Go take your shower. Mr. Zimmerman is picking us up in forty-five minutes. I hope you don't mind the backseat—Wanda is going to be up front. Oh, he said he'd be honored if Wishbone came along, too," Ellen said.

"Yes, Mom." Joe sighed as he headed for the stairs. "Come on, Wishbone. You can help me pick out a clean shirt."

"There's going to be a feature film, cartoons, and a serial," Ellen called up after him. "I think you'll like the show!"

Wishbone's evening was starting out great. "This is the life, Joe!"

He was between Joe and Ellen in the backseat of the Hudson, his paws resting against the back of the front seat. He had a great view of the screen between Horace and Wanda. Everyone had gigantic tubs of hot, buttered popcorn, and soft-drink cups large enough for a Jack Russell terrier to bathe in.

Wishbone nudged his friend with his head. "You know, a couple of pizza slices would have been perfect, but I guess you can't have everything. This is so neat!" Joe rubbed his dog's head with one hand, while he ate popcorn with the other.

69

Sam and David were in a big old Buick Roadmaster parked to their left. Wishbone could just see them through the back window of the other car. *Tough luck, kids,* he thought. *Not everyone rates a convertible, I guess!*

As soon as it had gotten dark, the show had started. The cartoons had erupted in an explosion of color. Wishbone had to admit that it certainly was better than watching them on TV.

And the serial! Chapter Three of *Zorro's Fighting Legion!* Wishbone wanted to leap out of the car and onto the screen to help the black-masked and black-caped Zorro fight for justice in old California.

But the cartoons and the serial had been nothing compared to the feature film! Wishbone's tail was wagging so hard that it seemed it might vibrate right off his body.

"A great dog story—*Old Yeller!*" Wishbone gazed at the screen with fascination as the western story unfolded. He thought to himself that, good as the star was, a Jack Russell terrier might have been better. "Hey, Joe! Do you know how I would go about getting a job in the movies? How far away is Hollywood, anyway?"

Joe scratched him between his ears and Wishbone sighed, settling down with his chin resting on his outstretched paws. Things were going just great. He didn't have to look around to know that the Moonlight Drive-In was practically perfect. The night air was filled with the smell of fresh paint, coming from the concession building and the ticket booth. All the trash from the parking lot had been collected in a big green garbage container. The newly painted screen gleamed.

Around the Hudson, the speaker posts all seemed

to have cars next to them filled with people munching on tubs of buttery-flavored popcorn and sipping soft drinks and thick, creamy shakes. The big screen dominated the clear night sky, and Wishbone sensed nothing scary lurking in the darkness—no long black limousines, and no tall, lean men with cold eyes and shark smiles.

A gigantic Old Yeller bounded across a western field. It seemed to Wishbone that the heroic canine was looking right out of the screen directly at the audience. Wishbone heard a low "woof!" from outside the Hudson. He knew immediately that it was timid old Shemp the sheepdog, getting an early start in the clean-up department—hoping to locate a tossed-away hot dog or two.

Go get 'em, pal, Wishbone thought dreamily. The

Jack Russell terrier settled down closer to his own personal friend and sighed with contentment.

Yep, it looks like things are finally starting to go right for Gladys Glendower and the wonderful old Moonlight Drive-In!

Chapter Six

Thinking that he was spending all his time lately at the Moonlight Drive-In cleaning up, Joe asked his mother, "This should be the last cleaning day, don't you agree, Mom?"

Ellen Talbot, behind the wheel of the family's Ford Explorer, barely glanced sideways at her son. "It ought to be," she replied. "Wanda thought it would take a full week, but I can't think of anything else you can possibly do to fix up the place. Can you?"

Joe considered that remark for a moment. It was Wednesday, and they were driving out to the Moonlight—again—to put the finishing touches on the drive-in. "I can't think of a thing," he said. "By now all the paint will be dry, the concession building will be spotless, and all the garbage is on its way to the recycling center. The old wiring has all been replaced. Sam, David, and I have helped out with all the small kinds of repair work, including putting the lock back on the office window."

"Oh," Ellen said. "Is that window how the vandal got inside the concession building to pour oil all over everything?"

"I think so," Joe told her. He explained that Mrs. Glendower had noticed the broken lock only the day before. It appeared to close properly, but she discovered to her surprise that the catch had been either filed off or sawed off with a hacksaw, so the latch did not work.

Mrs. Glendower had been so upset that she had called the police, and Officer Krulla had responded. Unfortunately, as he pointed out, so much cleaning had been going on that they had no hope of getting a single set of fingerprints. He just advised her to replace the lock. Joe and David had done so.

Joe looked back at Wishbone, who was sitting in the backseat with an alert expression. "Wishbone never gets tired of helping out. I think that's because people share their lunches with him!"

Ellen chuckled, and they made the turn into the Moonlight Drive-In's parking lot. Joe noticed how bright the ticket building looked in the sun, and how the trim of the concession building was as crisp and shiny as new. The really big job that he and his friends had helped with was the repainting of the screen, and that gleamed in the sunlight. Not many cars were around today, and only a few kids were helping out.

"Too bad Sam and David couldn't come today," Joe said as Ellen parked next to Mr. Zimmerman's Hudson Hornet.

"Well, there really can't be much left to do," Ellen replied.

They got out of the Explorer, and Joe held the

door open for Wishbone. He leaped out, sniffed the ground, and went speeding toward the concession building. Joe took a deep breath himself, noticing that the smell of paint was fading. He and Ellen walked across the asphalt to the concession building.

Joe narrowed his eyes. Ahead of them, Wishbone had stopped dead in his tracks and stood with his head lowered, looking as if he were angry.

"What's wrong, boy?" Joe hurried to catch up to Wishbone. As he came around the corner of the concession building, he saw Mrs. Glendower and her sixteen-year-old niece, Kelly, standing near the balding Mr. Penny, the city building inspector. Joe felt his heart sink. Mrs. Glendower was crying again, and Kelly, dressed in jeans and a work shirt, wore a very grim expression.

"B-but we've *done* all that," Mrs. Glendower was saying. "We worked so hard—"

"I'm really sorry, Mrs. Glendower," replied Mr. Penny in a frustrated voice. "Rules are rules, and regardless of what you think of them, you absolutely have to obey them."

Joe approached Kelly and said, "Hi."

She barely looked at him.

Mr. Penny held out his clipboard. "Now, these electrical repairs, for instance. What you don't seem to realize is that to meet the city code, they have to be carried out by licensed and bonded electricians—"

"But they were," Mrs. Glendower said miserably. "Mr. Zimmerman's friend Adam Tristram owns an electrical-repair company, and his work crew volunteered to do the labor."

Mr. Penny shook his head impatiently. "No, no, Mrs. Glendower, please hear me out. Now, Mr. Tristram's crew may be fully licensed in their home city, but they're from out of state. To meet the technical portion of the law, they have to be licensed and bonded in *this* state, and they're not. So I'm afraid I can't certify these repairs as having been done until you have the work checked out by a properly licensed local electrician. Now, the list includes a few more things—"

"We've heard enough, Mr. Penny," Kelly said. She turned to her aunt. "Aunt Gladys, you can see what's happening. They're just not going to let you open. I think you may as well give up. Somebody just doesn't want you running the Moonlight Drive-In."

Mrs. Glendower lowered her eyes. "I hate to disappoint everyone," she murmured. "Especially after they were all so nice about volunteering to help get the place in shape."

Kelly put an arm around her aunt's waist. "I know, I know. But you can get a lot of money from the Mega-Mall corporation for this land. That would be enough for you to live well for the rest of your life. Maybe you should consider selling." After a pause, Kelly said, "You'd never have to worry about money again if you did sell the drive-in."

Joe hoped that Mrs. Glendower wouldn't agree. He could certainly see Kelly's point, but Mrs. Glendower was right. People in Oakdale—including Joe—were really pulling for the Moonlight's owner to reopen and make a success of the business venture.

"What is going on here?" At the sound of Wanda Gilmore's voice, Joe turned in surprise. Dressed in colorful denim overalls and a floppy-brimmed purple sun hat, she came marching toward the assembled group. Horace Zimmerman was tagging along at her heels, trying hard to keep up. Joe felt Wishbone lean against his leg, and he reached down to scratch his buddy's head reassuringly.

Ellen, who had been standing with her arms crossed, said, "Wanda, Mr. Penny says some of the repairs haven't been carried out properly."

Wanda's eyes grew wide. "What! After all our hard work! Really, William Penny, you should be ashamed of yourself!"

Mr. Penny clutched his clipboard protectively to his chest. "Now, now, Miss Gilmore, rules are rules." When Wanda just stood and glared at him, he cleared his throat and said, "I'll admit you people have done a

lot out here—quite a lot, really. But you must know that the building codes mean more than just a few coats of fresh paint and a little garbage pickup. There are all sorts of matters of safety and—"

"What are they?" Wanda demanded.

Mr. Penny coughed. "The paving, for example. In places, the asphalt is badly cracked. Now, that could lead to someone tripping and breaking a leg. Then, too, there's some question about the wiring repairs. We haven't done a sanitary inspection of the kitchen and food-service area. And I have a whole long list of new concerns—"

"William," said Wanda in a threatening tone of voice, "we've made arrangements to take care of the paving. That should be done tomorrow. Now, you're mentioning new concerns. Exactly where are all these complaints coming from?"

"Well, they're concerns that have to be—" Mr. Penny stopped abruptly and blinked. "What did you just ask?"

Joe thought that Mr. Penny looked a little sheepish, as if Wanda's sudden question had caught him off guard and was somewhat embarrassing to him.

Wanda stared coldly at Mr. Penny and repeated, "Exactly where are all these complaints coming from? We already went over your whole list, and I thought we did a satisfactory job in meeting the city code. So where are all of these new items coming from?"

"We . . . uh . . . I have my sources," Mr. Penny said. His face grew red. "Now, Mrs. Glendower, Miss Gilmore, please don't get me wrong. I like movies just as much as anyone else, and I'm really sorry about all this. However, I can't make an exception to all the rules and regulations just because I happen to like this place, and—"

"William," Wanda said patiently, "you haven't answered my question. It's that MegaMall outfit, isn't it?"

Mr. Penny sighed. "We keep getting anonymous tips," he said.

Joe narrowed his eyes, remembering the Ellery Queen mystery he was reading. *The Roman Hat Mystery* included some anonymous tips, too. In it, Ellery Queen, the brilliant son of Inspector Richard Queen of the New York City Police Department, became an amateur detective to help out his father. The central mystery in the story was the puzzling murder of a man named Monte Field. He was killed while attending a show called *Gunplay* at the Roman Theater.

Ellery's problem was not that he was without suspects—in fact, he had *too many* suspects, a whole theater audience full. The mystery was complicated even more due to the fact that different witnesses gave him conflicting stories about just what was going on. The trick that Ellery learned was to discover which clues were real, and which ones were only distractions. To clarify that, Ellery had to consider the psychology of the witnesses—some of them lied because they were afraid, and others were mistaken about what they thought they had seen and heard.

Ellery had to consider the psychology of the murdered man, too. Mr. Monte Field was a hard-working businessman with a love of gossip. He never took a vacation. Ellery had been the one to decide that Field had come to the theater not to see the play, but to meet someone from whom he hoped to get money. The goal of gaining money fit his psychological profile—the way he thought and behaved—while attending a play did not. Joe wondered if he could spot some similar clues and patterns in the Moonlight Drive-In case.

Joe asked, "How did you get the tips, Mr. Penny?"

Mr. Penny looked around in surprise. "Why, unsigned notes were slipped under the front door of City Hall," he said. "Up until yesterday. Then, yesterday, someone tossed an envelope into my car. I found it this morning, and that's why I decided I'd better pay another visit out here."

"What was in the envelope?" Wanda asked.

Mr. Penny flipped through the papers on his clipboard. "This note."

Joe craned his neck to see. Someone had very carefully printed a note in squared-off letters that looked as if they had been drawn with the aid of a ruler. Joe couldn't read the entire note, but he could make out part of it:

> YOU SHOULD CHECK THE LICENSES OF THE ELECTRICIANS. HAVE THE GRILL SURFACES BEEN CHECKED FOR BACTERIA? ARE THE TEMPERATURE CONTROLS ON THE OVEN AND STOVE UP TO STANDARD? HOW ABOUT THE CRACKED ASPHALT? IS THAT A HAZARD TO PEDESTRIAN TRAFFIC? MAYBE YOU SHOULD...

Wanda said, "I can't believe you'd take the word of someone who doesn't have the decency to sign their note on a matter as important as this! As I said earlier, we went over your list, checked off every item that was completed, and did a good job."

Mr. Penny sighed and tucked the clipboard under his arm. "Miss Gilmore, these are legitimate complaints. I simply can't license the Moonlight Drive-In for regular business.

"Now, I know how much this place means to you, Mrs. Glendower, and that's why I made this special trip. Believe it or not, I really want to help you out, so I thought I'd warn you about these issues. The building inspector's office isn't completely heartless, you know. I think I can report that you've made enough initial progress to open for general film-showing business, but you will need to wait to open the concession stand. And you will have to hire a local, licensed electrician to come in and inspect and approve all the repairs and rewiring."

Joe wasn't really listening. He was thinking about that strange note. He didn't know a lot about police investigation work, but he strongly suspected that a note printed like the one Mr. Penny had received would make it impossible for a handwriting expert to analyze it and discover who had written it.

The unsigned note is very suspicious, Joe thought. *In fact, it's the kind of clue that Ellery Queen would jump on. The important thing isn't what's written in the note—it's the fact that the writer went to so much trouble to make the note untraceable. Now, if I could only figure out who would do that. . . .*

Wishbone nudged Joe. "Hey, Joe. *I* have some ideas about who might be behind those mysterious notes. Let me tell you about the car I noticed that first night as it went by the drive-in—the car with a certain Mr. Harry Bliss almost certainly riding inside it. . . ." Wishbone looked up and saw that Joe wasn't listening. He seemed wrapped up in his own thoughts.

With a shake of his head, Wishbone walked away from the group, his nose to the ground. He strongly suspected that Harry Bliss was somehow behind those anonymous tips.

Mr. Bliss has an excellent motive for causing trouble, thought Wishbone. *Now, if I can only sniff out some real proof that he's been snooping around here, maybe that would get Joe's attention. Let's see . . .*

For a few minutes, Wishbone nosed around the edges of the parking lot. Finally, he sneezed and sat down. "This will be a challenge! We Jack Russell terriers are excellent hunters, but no one ever thought of breeding a dog to track cars. If Harry Bliss and his companion have actually been sneaking onto the premises, they didn't get out of that big black limo of theirs, so they left no scent."

Wishbone stretched out in the grassy play area, enjoying the warmth of the afternoon sun on his fur. *Let me think about this. The note seemed pretty detailed. I don't think Mr. Bliss could have checked all that stuff out from the backseat of his car, yet I can't smell any trace of him. Hmm. Could he have someone working for him? A spy on the inside, maybe?*

It was a frustrating line of thought—how do you prove this theory one way or the other? He noticed that Mr. Penny was climbing into his own car, a tan sedan. Mr. Penny started the car and then drove away to the exit. Ellen drove off, also.

Wishbone sighed and laid his head on his paws. If only he could—

Suddenly he sat up, every bit of his keen canine senses on the alert. His ears perked up. From beyond the wooden fence that stretched around the drive-in, he had heard a sound—a very familiar one!

As soon as Mr. Penny had turned his car onto the road, followed by Ellen, Wishbone heard the engine of another car start. That car must have been parked on the shoulder of the road, just beyond the fence and out of sight from the Moonlight Drive-In. After the car's engine purred to life, it quietly rolled away, following Mr. Penny's sedan.

Running to alert Joe to the intruder, Wishbone thought, *It's him! It's him! I'd recognize that limo's sinister catlike sound anywhere!*

The sound was that of the sleek car that always transported Mr. Harry Bliss.

Chapter Seven

"Wishbone! Stop tugging at my shoe!" Joe looked down and decided that his buddy looked apologetic. He knelt and ruffled Wishbone's ears. "Later, boy. Right now I need to listen to what Miss Gilmore's saying."

"Plumber! Plumber! Where's my plumber?" Wanda Gilmore stood on W. C. Fields's old golf cart, her voice cutting through the summer morning at the Moonlight Drive-In like scissors cutting through a sheet of metal.

A stocky man in gray work clothes glanced around, as if hoping she was looking for some other plumber, before he finally raised his hand.

"Oh, there you are! Wonderful!" Wanda stuck her reading glasses on the tip of her nose and stared at the sheaf of official-looking papers in her right hand. "Section forty-six, paragraph thirteen, sub-paragraph . . . Aha! We need you to check out the ladies' room in the concession building. Mr. Penny says there's something wrong with the drains in the sinks there." The plumber hustled past her on his way to check out the job site. Wanda smiled politely and then returned to her papers.

"Electricians! Do we have a *local* electrician? Oh, hi, Ms. Martin. I have a little inspection job for you to take care of. . . ." Before long, the Moonlight Drive-In was alive with a large supporting cast of volunteer helpers. Eleven kids from school had come to pitch in, and half a dozen adults. Wishbone kept looking around. Joe thought he was trying to take in all the excitement at once.

Wanda was deep in conversation with a painter when Mr. Kepler, Sam's dad, drove up. Sam and David climbed out of his car.

Joe grinned and walked over, with Wishbone close beside him. "I thought you guys couldn't make it," he said.

David shrugged. "We both were able to change our plans so we could help. It's been fun working at the drive-in, so here we are again. What can we do?"

"I'm sure Miss Gilmore will have something in mind," Joe said with a grin.

"I'll go check," David said as he made his way over toward the golf cart.

Sam was shading her eyes and looking up at the screen. "We did a good job, didn't we?"

"Looks great," Joe agreed.

"Hey, Joe," a voice called out. Joe turned just in time to see David returning with three rakes. "Miss Gilmore says that the grass along the fence line needs raking. It's been cut, but now the clippings have to be collected and bagged."

"Okay," said Joe, as he took one of the offered rakes. "At least we should be finished with that in a decent amount of time."

David made a complete circle, pointing at the fence, which enclosed the entire drive-in. David laughed. "I don't think so. According to Miss Gilmore, there's about twelve years' worth of dead leaves and rubbish piled up along that fence. According to Mr. Penny, that's a code violation—it's a fire hazard or a health hazard, or just plain ugly or something. Anyway, we've got to get it all out of there."

"Might as well get started, then," Joe said. He, Sam, and David walked toward the fence area by the ticket booth.

Wishbone watched them go to take care of their chore. "Oh, well. Joe's got a job, and so do I—clue patrol!" And he bounded away across the lot.

Wishbone greeted the various licensed workers and volunteers. People grinned and even waved. *Treat people like you want to be treated, and they can be as friendly as dogs,* he thought happily. More than once, he zeroed in on a worker who was enjoying lunch, and often Wishbone persuaded the worker to share. There was plenty of food, but no clues.

The only dark spot on the day was Shemp. Try as he might, Wishbone just couldn't get the old sheepdog interested in helping. "Come on, Shemp, old pal! There are people having lunch! Bread crusts and bacon pieces! Potato chips! Come on!"

Shemp made one of his standard woofing noises. The big dog settled back down into the patch of warm sunlight.

Wishbone gave a shrug. "O-*kay* . . . tell you what, if anything comes up, I'll let you know. Wag something if any of this is getting through."

Shemp didn't move. Wishbone sighed and went back to work, inspecting the grounds.

At least Wishbone made no additional sightings of the creepy-looking black limo. He kept a careful ear on the road during his rounds anyway—just in case the long, sinister car might slither by.

In the late afternoon, a paving truck showed up, and a crew of workers began to pave over the cracks and holes in the parking lot with steaming-hot new asphalt. Wishbone sneezed at the strong smell of tar. All around him, people laughed and worked and cleaned and painted, slowly restoring the old drive-in to its former glory.

If only he could cheer up Shemp. The big dog seemed unusually shy.

Although all the work was proceeding well, Wishbone still had the sense that something else was going on that he couldn't quite smell. Occasionally, for no reason, the fur on his back would rise up. *I know something peculiar is happening, but I just can't seem to put my paw on it,* he thought. *Oh, well—maybe I just have overly suspicious fur.*

Toward the end of the day, Joe joined Sam, David, Miss Gilmore, and Mr. Zimmerman at the official opening night for paying customers of the Moonlight Drive-In. In fact, Mr. Zimmerman had bought tickets for Joe, David, and Sam.

"I'm really fond of the Hudson," apologized Horace Zimmerman over his shoulder. "But I've had it out and been driving it so much lately that I'm going to give it a rest. Tomorrow I'm treating it to a hand-waxing and detail job. I hope the Packard is acceptable to everyone. I mean, it isn't a convertible . . ."

"The Packard is fine, Horace," Wanda Gilmore said, adjusting her hat. "They are excellent automobiles. Everyone says so."

Joe grinned in the dark. Sam and David had joined him and Wishbone in the backseat of the massive green car, and there was still room to spare.

"Wow!" Sam said, looking around. "There sure are a lot of cars here tonight."

"Yeah," David responded, munching on his popcorn. "And the best thing is, this time they're all paying customers. That's gotta make Mrs. Glendower happy. Even with volunteer help, buying all the building and repair materials must have cost her quite a bundle."

The late-summer evening had turned cool, and Horace had provided blankets for his "passengers" to place over their laps. Wishbone lay wrapped up in one, only his head sticking out.

Mrs. Glendower had decided to show the *Zorro* serial again. Once more, Zorro was thundering across the huge screen on his black horse, the sound of hoof-beats pounding out of the speaker hanging on the Packard's front window frame. The sound wasn't stereo, but somehow everything seemed just right.

Wishbone wiggled next to Joe, who then reached down to scratch his ears. Wishbone looked around, his ears standing up straight and tense. Joe felt the little dog's body grow still next to him. The fur on his back rose up and bristled.

"What's wrong, boy?" Joe whispered. Sam heard Joe and glanced over at them.

"What's the matter with Wishbone, Joe?" Sam asked, also whispering.

Joe shook his head thoughtfully. "I don't know—all of a sudden he seemed tense and just started looking around."

Then before Joe could stop him, Wishbone jumped up from the seat and was staring out the back window of the Packard. A whine escaped from his throat and then he started to bark loudly.

"Wishbone!" Joe said. "Quiet, boy!" He was aware of people moving and shifting positions in several of

the cars around them, and he could see disapproving stares in the dark night. That didn't seem to bother Wishbone, though—he just kept barking. Joe tugged at Wishbone's leather collar. "You're interrupting the movie, Wishbone!"

"Really, Joe," Wanda said from the front seat. "If Wishbone won't behave, we're going to have to leave and miss the movie!"

"I'm sorry, Miss Gilmore. I don't know what in the world could be making him—"

"Hey, look! There's something wrong with the picture!" David cried, pointing at the flickering image up on the white screen. Joe turned away from his barking dog to look forward. Sure enough, the movie had become all splotchy, almost as if clouds were floating past the projector.

Or smoke . . .

Joe whipped around and stared at the distant projection booth. The booth was located on the top of the concession building—and that was exactly where the trouble was. Black smoke was billowing out of one of the building's windows. Joe opened the car door and jumped out, yelling, "The concession building is on fire!"

All over the parking lot, heads were turning and other voices taking up the cry. Wishbone scrambled out of the open door and raced across the parking lot.

Afraid of what might happen to Wishbone running through the dark in a lot full of cars, Joe ran after him. "Wishbone! Wait for us! Wishbone!"

Joe ran right behind Wishbone, and Sam and David followed closely behind him. Joe still held the blanket—he had kept his grip on it when he leaped out of the car. As he ran, Joe heard a dull whomping sound being repeated over and over, as if someone were beating an old carpet with a baseball bat. *That's Shemp barking,* he thought, as they raced around the side of the newly painted building.

They walked inside, and the concession building was full of smoke, which came pouring out of the counter and kitchen area. Shemp stood just outside the building, unable to enter. Gladys Glendower was in a far corner, yelling into a telephone. Her niece, Kelly, was tugging at her arm.

". . . yes, yes! The Moonlight Drive-In—on the outskirts of town! We've got a bad fire! You've got to come quickly!" She looked over and saw the kids standing, stunned, across from her.

"She won't leave! Help me get her out of here!" Kelly said urgently. "The whole place is about to burn down!"

Joe could see that the fire had spread all across the floor.

Wanda and Mr. Zimmerman arrived. Wanda took Mrs. Glendower outside.

"We can try to keep it under control until the fire-fighters come!" Joe yelled, trying to be heard over the noise of the fire—the crackling and popping made it difficult. "Kelly, get the fire extinguisher—bring it over, quick!"

"Are you crazy?" Kelly shouted. "The fire isn't just in here, but in the storage room. Get out now!"

Sam dashed past her, toward a fire extinguisher hanging on the wall. Mr. Zimmerman looked for something to extinguish the flames. Joe realized then that he was still holding the blanket.

"David, help Mr. Zimmerman find something to fight the fire!" Joe ran to the kitchen. He soaked his blanket with water in the sink. Then he went toward the fire. The heat was intense, and knee-high flames blazed along half the floor. From behind him, Joe heard Wishbone's barks.

Coughing, Joe swung the heavy, soaked blanket onto the worst area of the flames. They flew backward for a moment, then seemed to blow right back. Part of the floor was a solid mass of fire as he heaved the blanket up and down, again and again.

"Step aside, Joe!" Sam shouted. She raced toward him with the fire extinguisher and sent a steady spray

of thick white foam into the flames. "We've got the fire out in the storage room!"

David and Mr. Zimmerman located a hose that was connected to a water faucet just outside the door, and they dragged it inside. David shot water over a stack of cardboard boxes next to the door.

"Don't spray the water on the fire!" Joe yelled, as he pointed to some oil cans on the floor. "It's an oil fire—you'll just spread the flames!"

"Right!" David shouted back. "But we can wet down the other stuff to keep it from catching fire!"

"It's dying down!" Sam gasped. The fire extinguisher was doing the trick. As Joe watched, the fire gradually let up until the last licks of flames subsided. The tiles where the fire had been burning were now a blackened mess. Choking smoke filled the air inside, and continued to billow out the door.

Outside, in the distance, sirens wailed in the night and flashing red lights raced toward the Moonlight Drive-In.

A half-hour later, a weary Joe saw the firefighters come out of the concession area and begin to pack up their equipment. The fire chief stood in the doorway and motioned for Joe and the others to come in. "It's safe," he said. "Good job with the extinguisher, young lady. You acted quickly. The fire certainly could have been a lot worse if you hadn't thought to use it." He wiped his forehead with his slicker sleeve.

Once inside, Joe saw that everything in the

concession building was covered with greasy soot, and heavy smoke still hung in the air.

The chief looked around, nodding. "There's no structural damage—they built these old concession buildings out of cinder blocks and bricks. The ceiling could fall in, but the walls would still remain standing." He slapped a wall approvingly. "This is good solid work."

Joe, Sam, David, and Mr. Zimmerman stood slumped against the far wall, exhausted. The fire chief had been very generous in his praise of them all.

Joe looked around the place sadly. The newly painted concession building was now grimy, sooty, and soaked, and the entire place smelled strongly of smoke. The floor was drenched and streaked with muck, and everything was a complete mess. All that hard work renovating for nothing!

"Do you know what started it all, Chief?" Wanda asked in a tired voice. Horace Zimmerman, his well-tailored suit blackened with smoke, walked up to Wanda and stood behind her, awkwardly patting her on the shoulder. All Wanda's usual enthusiasm seemed to have drained out of her.

"Oh, that's the easy part, Miss Gilmore. My people found a frayed electrical cable lined up against the wall in that storage room. It must have become overloaded, and that's what started the fire."

"It must have been the extension cord to the lamp," Gladys Glendower said in between sobs. Her niece, Kelly, stood next to her, her arms protectively around her aunt's shoulders. "But I didn't think it was frayed. I would have noticed that!"

Kelly said, "Aunt Gladys, we know the fire wasn't your fault."

Mrs. Glendower shook her head. "Oh, my poor Moonlight! What are we going to do now? How am I ever going to open the drive-in?"

"Well, maybe you didn't notice the bad condition of that extension cord," the fire chief said. "But what has me puzzled is why the blaze spread so fast."

Joe said, "Someone *meant* it to—that's why."

Everyone turned and stared at him.

The fire chief wrinkled his forehead. "What?"

Joe stood up. When he spoke next, he couldn't keep the anger out of his voice. "That extension cord wasn't frayed. It was fine! I helped clean this place up, and I know it was all right. Someone must have deliberately cut and frayed the cord. And I'll bet somebody poured oil all around so the fire would spread really fast!"

"Oil was found on the floors, but the popcorn-oil cans were probably knocked over when you were trying to beat out the fire," the fire chief said.

"I don't think so," Joe said. "The oil wasn't stored against that wall in the storage room."

The fire chief looked grim. "So, you're saying someone deliberately tried to burn down the concession building," he said. "That's arson—a very serious crime. But you may be right. Now that I think back, the cord did look suspicious. Hmm . . . Let's review what we know. The fire began in the storage room, started by a frayed electrical cord. The spilled oil in the storage room ignited and went into the concession area. That's why the fire spread so fast—the oil trailed from the storage room into the concession area."

"But that's impossible!" said Gladys, still cradled in her niece's arms.

"Not at all, ma'am. Once the fire got started—"

Mrs. Glendower cried, "No! No! You don't understand! Joe's absolutely right about the oil. It isn't stored in the storage room! It's all kept in metal cabinets in the concession area next to the popcorn machine, so it's in a convenient location!"

Wanda went over to Mrs. Glendower. "Gladys, are you sure? I mean, couldn't the delivery people have made a mistake and put the oil in the storage room?"

"No, Wanda! It's all the way on the other side of the concession counter from the popcorn machine! It would have taken forever to go get more of it when we ran low!"

"And if Joe's right about the cord, he's right about something else," Sam said. "This *is* arson. Someone deliberately set fire to the place."

Joe nodded. "This is very similar to that other prank with spilled oil, but this time it's become much more serious. The vandal's getting really dangerous. People could have been hurt badly in this fire."

Wishbone felt proud of Joe. The fire chief was taking Joe's theory seriously. "Good investigative work, Joe! You've got a great head on your shoulders!" Then Wishbone glanced at Shemp. The big dog was a picture of canine dejection. He was trembling, too, as if half-terrified.

96

The shaggy old sheepdog lumbered to his feet and went over to where Kelly and her aunt were standing.

Wishbone sighed. "Why is Shemp so scared and unhappy? Well, right now I don't have time to worry about Shemp." His sharp canine mind was still filled with questions about the fire.

Who had set the mysterious fire? Did someone have it in for Kelly and her aunt? And could that someone be connected with MegaMall?

Chapter Eight

The next day, Thursday, Wishbone lay at the foot of Joe's bed, thinking things over. Joe had left the Ellery Queen story he was reading on the bed, and Wishbone rested his head on the book. Wishbone could not help reflecting that, in stories, things were neater and easier than they were in real life. A writer could give his fictional detective exactly the right amount of important clues to figure out a mystery.

That's fine for fictional detectives, Wishbone thought. *What about real life? That's when things get hard!* He stretched and yawned. Joe was out, and Ellen was at the library working. He was bored, and he was getting nowhere chasing the puzzle around in his head, like a pesky cat that always was about one set of paws ahead of him.

Wishbone jumped off the bed and headed to the kitchen. *Maybe a little fresh air will get my usually sharp canine mind working at full blast,* he mused. He went out into the yard. It was a day of broken clouds, with blue sky showing through. Wishbone took a deep sniff of the morning air. Nothing unusual there—just the normal, everyday odors of Forest Avenue.

Wishbone paced. Joe had been talking to him about the Ellery Queen mystery he was reading, and Wishbone thought that Ellery Queen had a good point. Sometimes the best clue to a puzzle might not be a footprint or a tiny fiber that could be peered at under a microscope. Sometimes the real tipoff might be in the way a person thought and behaved—the psychological clue, as Joe had called it.

O-kay, thought Wishbone. *Someone is playing mean and dangerous tricks at the drive-in. Someone set fire to the concession building. Now, who would do that?*

Wishbone trotted around the yard, then finally settled beside the back door. He closed his eyes to try to make it a little easier to think clearly. Before he knew it, he had drifted off into a deep morning nap.

Joe began to feel more and more that the only activity he was doing at home was sleeping. He was practically living at the Moonlight Drive-In. Wanda simply would not give up. The concession-building repairs began, again.

Since Mrs. Glendower was running dangerously low on cash, the workers who came forward to help make the fire repairs were all volunteers. There were fewer people available to help.

Joe, David, and Sam were given scrub-up duty.

They began the difficult job of cleaning and removing the greasy layers of black soot from some of the walls, floors, and ceilings in the concession building. The building also required replacement of surfaces that had been destroyed, new wiring, and, of course, repainting. After they had been working for more than three hours, Joe said, "I don't know about you two, but I'll be glad when we finish cleaning."

"You said it," David agreed immediately.

Joe looked at the concession area they had scrubbed so far. The ceiling was clean, though it, too, would need repainting. On two walls, the heat from the fire had raised blisters.

The other two walls were not seriously damaged by the fire, but their surfaces were still caked with grime. Joe rolled up his sleeves and hefted a fresh bucket of warm, sudsy water. "Well, at least the two blistered walls we've finished were the worst ones to clean," he said. "I'll go get some more water."

"Personally," Sam said, grunting, as she scrubbed away at a big black blotch in one corner of the room, "I'm glad that we finished the floors. They were the worst."

Joe lugged the heavy bucket to the big sink in the custodian's closet, behind the kitchen. He dumped out the greasy gray water, rinsed the bucket with steaming, fresh hot water, then refilled it and added more industrial-strength detergent.

As Joe dragged the fresh bucket of water out of the custodian's closet, he heard a familiar voice. "You don't understand," it was saying. "I'm not here to gloat. I just wanted to ask if you had considered the offer."

Joe recognized the voice almost instantly. It belonged to Harry Bliss—one of Joe's main suspects. This was a chance to investigate. Thinking of Ellery Queen, Joe wondered if Harry Bliss wanted the Moonlight property badly enough to risk other people's lives. Would that fit his psychology?

Setting the bucket down, Joe walked through the kitchen and toward the concession counter. On the far side, Mr. Bliss stood, with his assistant, Ms. Corwin, at his elbow.

Bliss said to Mrs. Glendower, "I heard about your trouble here. I thought I'd stop by and make sure that you hadn't changed your mind, that's all. I don't want you to think of me as your enemy." He sighed and turned to Ms. Corwin. "Maybe we should show Mrs. Glendower the new papers we've drawn up."

"Yes, sir."

As Joe watched, Ms. Corwin opened her slim briefcase and took out a thick legal document in a pale blue binder. Mr. Bliss took the bound papers from her and opened them up.

"Now," Mr. Bliss said to Mrs. Glendower, "I've been in touch with MegaMall's home office, and I've explained your great reluctance to sell. We really feel strongly that this is a prime location for a mall, Mrs. Glendower. I'm authorized to . . . well, forget the original offer. This is what MegaMall is willing to pay you now, today, for this property."

He handed the paperwork to Mrs. Glendower.

Joe heard her gasp.

"This is double what you offered before!" she said.

"That's right." Mr. Bliss extended his hand to Mrs.

Glendower. He was holding a gleaming black pen. "So why don't you just sign? Then we'll gladly take care of the rest."

Joe swallowed hard. He stepped forward. "I don't think you should," he said to Mrs. Glendower.

Mr. Bliss and Ms. Corwin were both startled by Joe's forceful remark. Mr. Bliss turned his cold eyes on Joe. "Excuse me, young man, but I don't see how this is any of your business."

Joe's heart was pounding. He felt an irrational fear of this man with the frosty stare and chilly voice. Still, Joe said, "I don't think it's fair at all to force Mrs. Glendower to sell the theater if she doesn't want to."

"Force?" Mr. Bliss sounded truly surprised. "I'd never force anyone to do anything! If Mrs. Glendower sells her property to my company, it will be because she *wants* to, and because MegaMall's new offer is a most generous one."

Mrs. Glendower began: "I . . . I don't know . . ."

The door to the concession stand opened. Wishbone rushed in, glanced at Mr. Bliss, and scampered to Joe's side. Behind Wishbone came Kelly and Wanda, both of them wearing determined expressions. "Gladys, don't you sign a thing!" warned Wanda.

Mr. Bliss sighed. "Well, it's clear that Mrs. Glendower needs time to think things through," he said. "I'll be in touch. Come, Ms. Corwin."

Joe looked at the woman and realized for the first time that she was holding something besides her briefcase. She also had with her a very small camera. As the two of them went outside, Mr. Bliss pointed at something, and she photographed it.

"Look at that!" Wanda said. "Coming in here and harassing you! I'll just bet that woman is taking pictures of things they're going to report as building code violations! Gladys, don't you dare sign anything!"

"I haven't, Wanda," Mrs. Glendower said.

Wanda looked around. "I think," she said, "someone from the MegaMall Corporation is coming out here and causing all the problems. Well, we can't prove anything, and we still have a lot to do, so let's get back to work."

Joe turned and saw that Sam and David had come out of the storage room, which they were now cleaning, to hear what was going on. He shook his head at them, and they returned to their tasks.

"Joe," Sam said, as she changed brushes and furiously began to attack a long streak of soot, "we overheard the conversation. Do you think Miss Gilmore's right? Was Mr. Bliss or someone else from MegaMall behind this fire?"

"I'm just not sure," Joe had to admit. "But I certainly don't know of anyone else who would have a reason to try to burn the place down. If MegaMall is behind the vandalism, it's going to be hard to prove. The company's got lots of money, and it must have thousands of people working for it."

"It may be too big a situation for us to handle," David said.

Joe shook his head. "It doesn't matter. Whoever's behind all this trouble shouldn't get away with it. Do you guys agree with me?"

"Sure," Sam said. "I don't want to see Mrs. Glendower or anyone else hurt."

"I'm with you, too," David said.

"Then we've got to think like Ellery Queen," Joe told them. He had already told them about the book he was reading, and they both nodded at once. Joe said, "From now on, we look for all kinds of clues—even the invisible ones. We have to be aware of the psychology of this crime. Someone's not behaving in any ordinary way. We're going to make it our job to find out who that is."

A little after five that afternoon, Ellen came out to drive the kids home. They stowed their coveralls in the custodian's closet. Then Joe opened the door of the concession stand and found himself facing Ms. Martin, the local, licensed electrician whom Mr. Penny had insisted check out the wiring.

Beneath her orange hard hat, Ms. Martin's freckled face was grim. "Where's Mrs. Glendower?" she asked, hitching up the tool belt that she wore around her yellow jumpsuit.

Joe pointed toward the office. "She's in there. What's wrong?" he asked.

"Plenty."

"Ready to go, Joe?" Ellen asked from the doorway.

Joe raised his hand. "Wait just a minute, Mom. Something's up."

David groaned. "Something *else?*"

Sam said, "Shh!"

Ms. Martin called out to Mrs. Glendower. The woman came hurrying out of the office. She and Ms.

Martin strode across the parking lot. Joe, Ellen, Sam, David, and Wishbone hurried behind.

At the front row of speakers, Ms. Martin reached over and lifted one of the aluminum boxes off its post. "Look at this," she said, and gave the black speaker wire a very slight tug.

Wanda arrived and looked on with a frown.

Joe grimaced, knowing that what he saw was going to upset Mrs. Glendower greatly. The wire to the speaker was loose. It slipped right out and dangled in the electrician's hand.

She tilted her hard hat back on her head. "The whole first row is like that," she said. "Someone used wire cutters, snipped the wires, then shoved them back into the sockets just enough so they appeared to be intact. But they won't work, of course. So, with the front row out, all the speakers in the lot are out, because this is a serial wiring setup. All the boxes have to be taken apart and the wires reconnected. It'll take a good three or four hours to finish them all."

"They weren't like this yesterday," said Mrs. Glendower, turning the speaker box over in her hands. "We checked the system just last night."

"They weren't like that early this morning, either," Wanda said. "I know, because one of the speakers had fallen off, and I picked it up and put it back in position. The wire certainly hadn't been cut, or it would have come loose."

Joe's heart felt like lead. Cutting the wires was another malicious act of vandalism, and that was bad enough in itself.

Whoever had cut the wires had to have done it

that very day. That meant the vandal wasn't Mr. Bliss, or Ms. Corwin, or even their driver. Mr. Bliss and Mega-Mall were on everyone's list as suspects. The limo was watched carefully by the fix-up crew whenever it appeared at the drive-in. Being watched that carefully, especially today, the MegaMall people would not have had a chance to cut the wires. It had to be someone on the fix-up crew.

It had to be someone who Joe would have been certain was a good friend to Mrs. Glendower.

Chapter Nine

"Yes, Wanda," Horace Zimmerman said to Wanda Gilmore as he pulled the Hudson up to the Moonlight Drive-In's concession building. Actually, Joe realized, Wanda was doing all the talking, and Horace was just voicing his occasional agreement. Joe and Wishbone sat in the backseat with Sam and David, not saying anything at all. The Fix-Up Project had extended into Friday—day five.

"I just think the police should be doing more, that's all."

"Wanda, the police arrived soon after the fire started and are doing the best they can. They were also contacted regarding the cut wires. They are on the case," Zimmerman said.

"I mean, that's why we pay taxes, isn't it? They should be doing *something.*" Wanda continued as if Mr. Zimmerman had not spoken.

"Yes, Wanda."

"Stop agreeing with me, Horace."

"Yes, Wanda." Horace frowned and seemed to change his mental gears. "The police probably have a hard time making any progress when all the clues tend to burn up."

"The speaker wires didn't burn up," Wanda said triumphantly.

Horace sounded almost fatherly when he said, "Wanda, they can't just arrest everyone in Oakdale who owns a pair of wire cutters. They'd have to build a new jail."

Horace got out of the Hudson and walked around the front of the car to open the door for Wanda. "We just have to hope they can find out who's doing all these terrible things before it's too late."

"They should arrest Harry Bliss—that's what they should do," Wanda said, adjusting her hat. "He's behind all this."

"I don't see how Mr. Bliss could be the culprit," Joe finally said from the backseat. Wanda turned toward him with a surprised look on her face. Joe added, "He just wouldn't have had the chance. We've seen him shortly before or after the acts of vandalism. And his clothes would have shown traces of oil—someone would have noticed, right? It would be a dead give-away, wouldn't it?"

"I don't know about all that, but I'm certain he doesn't want to help Gladys *or* the Moonlight!" Wanda said. Wishbone barked excitedly as he bounded from the seat to the ground. Wanda gestured toward him. "See, even Wishbone agrees with me!"

"Actually, I think he's just glad to see Shemp," Sam said, pointing. Sure enough, the large shaggy form of Shemp the sheepdog had come out of the concession building, moving as fast as he ever did—which, Joe thought, was *not very fast*—and came right up to Wishbone. Then they sat down on the asphalt together. To Joe, they looked as if they were waiting for something.

Horace brushed some imaginary lint from his immaculate suit. "I guess we need to find out what the plan is for today—the rest of the volunteers should be here any minute now. We're down to only a few."

"Gladys is keeping track of all that, Horace. . . . Ah, here she is! Gladys! Yoo-hoo! Gladys!"

Gladys Glendower was hurrying toward them much faster than Shemp had. She glanced nervously over her shoulder at the open door of the concession building. She yoo-hooed back at Wanda, with a smile that seemed entirely too bright, at least to Joe.

"Wanda! Horace! Kids! It's so great to see you! Why don't we all just go down to the screen and get things under way! I've got a list of—"

"Aunt Gladys!"

Gladys Glendower tensed as her niece, Kelly, hurried out of the building after her. She had a large, old-fashioned leather-bound ledger book tucked firmly under one arm. She did not look happy. When she spoke, Joe thought that she sounded almost like an adult scolding a child. "Aunt Gladys, you can't just keep running away from this! You've got to face facts!"

Mrs. Glendower gave her a weak smile. "Now, Kelly, dear, can't we discuss this later?"

Kelly rolled her eyes. "No, we *can't* discuss it later! 'Later' never gets here with you, Aunt Gladys! You just keep hurrying along as if everything was all right. Well,

it *isn't* all right!" She shoved the ledger book into her aunt's face. "You don't have any more money!"

"Kelly," said Wanda, smiling. "We don't have to worry about that. All the workers volunteered." She stopped walking as Kelly glared at her.

"No, we don't have to pay for the volunteers, Miss Gilmore," she snapped, her eyes flashing. "But my aunt *does* have to pay for the supplies, and she can't, because there isn't any money! Her checking account is down to its last hundred dollars. See!" She shoved the book at Wanda.

Joe glanced over Wanda's shoulder. She opened the ledger book. The pages were covered with small red-and-black-ink figures written in long columns. There was a lot more red ink than black.

Mrs. Glendower stared at Kelly. "But all the money that we made on opening night—"

"It barely paid for more paint and other materials to repair the damage the fire did to the concession building," Kelly said to her aunt. "It doesn't even come close to paying for the materials to rewire all the speakers in the front row!" Kelly looked at Wanda. "Electrical supplies cost money, Miss Gilmore, and my aunt barely has any left!"

Joe realized that Kelly was almost hysterical, close to tears. Probably, he thought, only her anger at the desperate financial situation kept her from breaking down entirely.

Horace Zimmerman gently took the ledger from Kelly and examined the figures. "I'm afraid Kelly's right. This doesn't look good," he said, his gaze moving up and down the pages. "I had no idea the Moonlight was requiring so much material." He turned to another page and his eyebrows shot up. "Oh, my—it actually gets worse, doesn't it?"

Kelly nodded vigorously, her face red. "That's what I keep trying to tell my aunt, but she won't listen to me! What's the use of recording figures if she just ignores them!"

"Kelly, you can't let this get to you." Gladys patted her arm awkwardly. "After everyone's helped so much, I can't just quit. We'll have to keep going on. If I have to, I can chip in some of my pension money—"

"Keep going on!" Kelly erupted, jerking away from her aunt. "How far do you think your pension money will go? Aren't you listening, Aunt Gladys? There isn't *any* money! There isn't *going* to be any money!" Then she turned her glare on Horace and Wanda. "And the rest of you! You're just encouraging her in this! Every time it looks as if she's going to listen to common sense, one of you comes running up with more painters or plumbers or electricians! Why don't you just leave us alone?"

"Kelly!" Mrs. Glendower's expression was one of deep shock.

"It's true—and you *know* it's true, Aunt Gladys! It's crazy to continue trying to keep this stupid place going! You shouldn't have to worry about whether it's going to burn up or fall down! If it wasn't for these people, you could unload this white elephant, make a nice profit, and relax! You could do whatever you want to do!"

Kelly yanked the ledger away from Horace and stormed back into the concession building, but not before everyone heard her crying.

Gladys stared after her, shocked and puzzled. "But I'm doing exactly what I want to be doing," she said. "I'm running the Moonlight." She looked at the others. "Kelly doesn't understand. For thirty years, my husband and I were so happy running this place. Both of us had day jobs, too, but running the drive-in was our true love. Kelly doesn't seem to realize how very little money I really need. After all—" Mrs. Glendower paused, and tears ran down her cheeks. "After all, what good is money if you're not happy?"

Joe glanced at Sam and David, who looked embarrassed. He didn't know what to say. Families, Joe had always thought, had to stick together. He felt sorry for Mrs. Glendower. Still, he thought, she had lots of friends to lean on for support. For a long moment, no one spoke. "I think we should go to work," Joe said.

Well, that was rough, Wishbone thought, glancing over at Shemp. The old sheepdog had slowly collapsed onto the ground, looking like a pile of discarded rag mops. "Uh . . . tell me, Shemp, old pal, has your girl always been this high-strung?"

Shemp gave one "woof," then laid his head down on his paws. *That's one depressed doggie,* Wishbone thought, shaking his head. *I'm lucky to have Joe as my human pal—he's almost as smart as a dog—and he can be taught. Hmm . . . speaking of Joe . . .*

"So what do we do now?" Joe said to Wanda, who still seemed stunned by the scene that had just unfolded.

"I don't know. Those figures are terrible! I had no idea costs for materials such as wire, wood, paint, and professional, licensed labor had increased so much! Poor Gladys. Where's she going to get all that money?"

Wishbone glanced over at the financially well-off Horace Zimmerman. *He's being strangely silent,* Wishbone thought. *You don't have much choice around Wanda, but Horace is being even more quiet than usual. Hmm . . . You can almost hear the mental gears turning in his head.* Wishbone watched as Horace seemed to come to some kind of conclusion. The man squared his shoulders and turned to Wanda.

"Wanda, the Oakdale Historical Society is a non-profit organization, isn't it?"

Wanda blinked at him. "What on earth does the society's tax status have to do with anything?"

"Just answer my question, Wanda . . . please?"

"Why, yes—yes, it is. But . . ."

Horace sighed, walked to his car, opened the

glove compartment, and took out a mobile phone. He seemed rather embarrassed about it.

"That's not exactly an authentic accessory, is it, Mr. Zimmerman?" David asked.

"No, David," Mr. Zimmerman said with a sigh. "But life is made up of compromises, and this is one of mine. All my cars have phones in them—I just keep them out of sight. Please don't say anything, Wanda— I know it isn't historically accurate. Neither are my plastic eyeglass lenses, and I'm not planning to give them up, either."

"I wasn't going to say anything, Horace."

Wishbone watched as Horace punched in a number. *You've got something up your sleeve, Mr. Z. That's something dogs can't do—no sleeves.*

"Hello . . . Jonathan? Zimmerman, here. How are we fixed for donations this year? . . . Really? Glad to hear it. Listen, a Miss Wanda Gilmore will call you today with a list. Take care of it, will you? . . . Great, knew I could depend on you, Jonathan. Best to Nancy and the kids. . . . Right. Good-bye."

"What was that all about? And just who am I supposed to be giving a list to, Horace Zimmerman?" Wanda said, standing with her hands on her hips.

"That was my accountant, Jonathan Quick. I don't just own restaurants, Wanda. I also own fifty-one percent of H. Z. Electrical Supply. If you get a list of the wiring Gladys needs and call this number—just punch 'recall'—Jonathan will see that it's donated through the historical society. Then you can use it to fix the speakers. It's not everything you'll need, but it's a start." Horace smiled. "And it's also a tax write-off for me, so it will be a good move for everyone involved."

Wishbone's tail thumped. "Smooth move, Mr. Z!"

"Horace J. Zimmerman, I could just kiss you!" Wanda said, clapping her hands together. "In fact, I think I will!" She planted a large kiss on his cheek.

"Things are really starting to look up, huh, Wishbone?" Joe said.

Wishbone licked his buddy's face. "They sure are, Joe! Right, Shemp?"

But Shemp wasn't looking at his friend. His hidden eyes stayed locked on the concession-building door, where Kelly had disappeared.

Saturday morning came around. Joe walked nervously beside Mr. Penny as they inspected the Moonlight Drive-In. Mr. Penny had his list, and Joe had a duplicate, on which he made penciled X's as Mr. Penny read off the list of repairs completed. "Speakers rewired—check. I understand your friend David assisted the electrician."

"Yes, and always under the supervision of Ms. Martin," Joe said. "She's a local, licensed electrician, you know."

Mr. Penny smiled. "I know. And David's a very talented young man. Let's see, the next item . . . Ticket-booth gutters repaired and cleaned—check. Playground swing-set chains and seats replaced—check."

Mr. Penny turned to walk around the edge of the lot, with Joe close behind. Over at the concession building, Gladys Glendower and Wanda Gilmore waited anxiously. Wanda had started to make the rounds with Joe and Mr. Penny, but her habit of pointing out the repairs before they reached them had led Mr. Penny to ask her gently to let only Joe come along instead.

Joe made another check mark as Mr. Penny said, "Parking-lot lights replaced—check." He continued walking. "Parking-slot lines repainted in standard yellow paint—check. Trash receptacles at proper intervals—check." Mr. Penny paused to look at four brand-new gates that had been placed in the wooden fence surrounding the theater. Above each one was an electric sign that said "Fire Exit." Mr. Penny nodded. "Fire exits appear to be sufficient. Uh . . . check."

Wishbone had been sniffing around one of the trash receptacles. Then he joined Mr. Penny and Joe, trotting along beside his pal, looking up hopefully. "I can't play right now," Joe told him in a low voice. "I know this is taking a long time, Wishbone."

Mr. Penny continued. "Cracks in asphalt at rows three, five, six, eleven, and twelve filled—check. Leaves and trash removed from fence line—check." Mr. Penny advanced, flipping through page after page as he did.

Horace Zimmerman sat behind the wheel of his car, resting. *He deserves a nap*, Joe thought. Mr. Zimmerman had donated the remaining electrical supplies needed, including the wire for the speakers.

Wanda, who had run a whole series of stories about the Moonlight Drive-In in the *Chronicle,* had called the area businesses that had supplied paint, lumber, and other items. All of them offered to refund the cost of their materials to Mrs. Glendower. Even Kelly had to admit that the Moonlight's financial figures were looking much healthier.

The concession building had been repaired and repainted. Now the Moonlight was looking very sharp, indeed. But the hard work wouldn't mean a thing if Mr. Penny wasn't satisfied. Finally, the little man stopped in front of the Hudson. He turned and his sharp eyes swept over the old drive-in one last time.

"Check and double check," he declared, making two final slashes with his pen. He surveyed the lot one last time, then slipped the pen into his suit pocket. "Mrs. Glendower?"

"Yes . . . Mr. Penny?" Gladys asked hesitantly.

"It is my duty as a duly appointed official of the city and county to inform you that the business establishment referred to as the Moonlight Drive-In Theater has successfully repaired the noted violations and is in full compliance with city, county, and state business regulations." Then he smiled and held out his hand. "Congratulations, ma'am, you're up to code."

Gladys stared at him for a moment, then broke into a huge smile and grabbed his hand. "Oh, thank you, Mr. Penny! You don't know what this means to me!"

"Thank goodness," Horace Zimmerman said almost breathlessly, leaning back against the Hudson's dark-leather seat. Joe whooped for joy, and Wishbone turned a triumphant backflip. Wanda beamed.

"You see, Gladys, I told you that everything would be all right!"

"Don't sell yourself short, Miss Gilmore," Mr. Penny said. "I would never have thought anyone could

have corrected that many violations in such a short period of time, but you folks did it. You're all to be congratulated—it's a job well done."

David and Sam gave each other a high-five, then rushed over to Joe. "We did it!" David yelled, laughing.

Joe smiled and nodded toward the concession building. The three friends walked toward it, away from Mrs. Glendower and the others. "We did it," Joe said in a low voice, "but there's one thing left undone. We still haven't caught the vandal. Until we do, there's no guarantee that whoever it is won't strike again."

"Hey," Sam said. "Look at Shemp. What's wrong with him?"

Joe turned. The sheepdog was sitting against the wall of the concession building, under the low window that opened into the office. He was whimpering softly.

Wishbone rushed over to see what was wrong with Shemp. He crouched low, his rear end held high and his tail wagging, in the universal dog signal for "Let's play!"

The mournful Shemp ignored him and continued to whine.

"What's wrong, boy?" Joe asked with concern. He went over to pet Shemp, but as he stooped, he heard another sound. He stopped with his hand hovering over Shemp's head. Then he whispered, "Let's go, Wishbone." He walked back to Sam and David. "Kelly is inside the office. I could hear her crying. That must be what's upset Shemp."

"Crying?" Sam asked. "But why? Her aunt's succeeded. She's saved the Moonlight."

"I don't know why she's crying," Joe said. "I think we should just leave her alone, though."

They walked away from the concession building, with Joe deep in thought. The police had all but stopped looking for the arsonist. They had no clues, no solid evidence. Joe thought once more of the Ellery Queen novel he was reading. Ellery had deduced that the murder victim, Monte Field, wasn't just a Wall Street businessman, as he appeared. His love of gossip and his greed had led him to become a blackmailer— and one of his blackmail victims had turned out to be the murderer. Through his cleverness, and his study of the psychology of all the potential blackmail victims in the theater, Ellery had solved the case.

There was just one thing wrong with a psychological clue, Joe thought—it never left any kind of trace for the police to examine.

The next morning Wishbone listened at breakfast as Ellen read a story aloud from the *Chronicle*. The article, written by Wanda, trumpeted the news about the Moonlight, along with a special announcement from the Oakdale Historical Society. In order to celebrate the drive-in's official approval, the society was going to sponsor, this upcoming Monday, a special "Drive-In Double-Feature Night." Admission would be only one dollar per car, and each customer would receive a free medium-size tub of popcorn, courtesy of *The Oakdale Chronicle*.

"Tomorrow night. Want to go?" Ellen asked Joe.

"Sure," Joe said. "School starts Tuesday, so it'll be an end-of-summer party. Maybe we'll see the next installment of the *Zorro* serial."

Wishbone saw that Ellen did not really want to go, although Joe did. *Aha!* he thought. *Joe's planning something. I can sense it. I know—maybe we're finally going to catch that Mr. Bliss in the act! I wish we could—maybe that would cheer up Shemp and turn him from a mournful mop into a regular dog at last.*

And on Monday night, everyone came. Wanda and Mr. Zimmerman again invited Joe, Sam, David, and Wishbone. The Antique Car Club turned out in force, along with what seemed like half the population of Oakdale. It was the perfect night to enjoy a drive-in movie—warm and clear, with no full moon to distract from the screen.

Everyone was set to have a great time. Wishbone

would have settled in happily, except that his friends seemed restless. Every few minutes, Sam, David, or Joe would hop out of the car to go to the restroom or go to find one of their friends in the sea of cars. Their behavior puzzled Wishbone.

Nobody but Wishbone noticed when Harry Bliss's sinister black limo purred through the entrance and parked at the back of the drive-in.

Chapter Ten

Wishbone watched the first feature with interest, but by the time the second feature—a movie called *Beach Blanket Bingo*—came on the big screen, he had decided to curl up next to Joe and have a nap. *Maybe next time there'll be a movie with a dog in it,* he thought.

Beside Wishbone, Joe stretched. "I think I'll go get a snack at the concession stand," he said for the sixth time. "Anybody want to come with me?"

Wishbone perked up instantly. "Snack? Snack? Count me in on that, Joe!"

David stretched, too. "I'll take a walk with you. How about you, Sam?"

"Sure," she said.

"I don't know why you kids are so restless tonight," Wanda said, shaking her head. "Watch for cars," Wanda warned.

"We will," Joe said.

They all climbed out of the backseat of the big car.

As they crossed the asphalt lot, Joe said, "Sam, did you check when you went to the rest room?"

"I sure did," Sam said. "Everything was fine."

Wishbone tilted his head. "What? Check for what? Something's going on here—I can smell it!"

David sounded a little nervous. "Everything was okay when I checked, too. Nothing unusual on the stake-out yet."

Wishbone's ears perked up. "Stake-out! I *knew* Joe had some plan! Way to go, Joe! You've been keeping an eye on Mr. Bliss, haven't you? My keen ears told me his limo parked exactly five rows behind us—"

Joe said to David, "This stake-out is very important. The police haven't been able to come up with anything, and I have the feeling that if anything serious is going to happen, it has to be tonight."

Sam's voice sounded uncertain when she said, "I don't know. Mrs. Glendower says Mr. Bliss has come back twice. He really wants her to sell the land. If a big outfit like MegaMall is behind all the trouble here, what can the three of us do about it?"

Wishbone sniffed. "Four of us, Sam—there are *four*. Don't forget the faithful dog!"

"First we have to make sure that we know exactly what's going on," Joe said. "And remember what I told you about the psychology of the vandal. It has to be someone who's determined to force the drive-in to close. Now, the pranks have been getting more and more serious, and fire seems to be part of the M.O.— the modus operandi, or the pattern of behavior in which the vandal operates.

"Now, if the vandal lets this big opening night

pass without causing any problems, it's going to be a missed opportunity for the culprit."

"And it just isn't right that someone continues to vandalize the drive-in. We can't stand by and watch someone wreck it," Sam said.

Joe agreed. "That's why we have to keep an extra-sharp eye on the concession buiding until the whole show is over." He opened the door.

Wishbone's stomach began to growl when he smelled the aromas in the night air: hot dogs, hamburgers, pizzas, and buttered popcorn, all mixed together. He licked his chops. Joe stood just inside the door, looking at Mrs. Glendower, who hovered behind the counter, a smile on her face.

"Yes, Joe?" she asked as the friends came inside, Joe in the lead.

"Hi," Joe said. "Uh . . . I thought Kelly was working behind the counter tonight. She was here the last time I came by."

"Oh, she wasn't feeling well," Mrs. Glendower said. "I had her lie down in the office."

Wishbone heard something. He looked back over his shoulder. David had let the concession-stand door close. But that was not the sound he heard. What attracted Wishbone's attention was so muffled that it might have been almost anything. Still, Wishbone was sure—well, he was *almost* sure—that he had heard a dog bark.

Except, since he had seen the movie before, he knew this one had no dogs in it.

Joe had assumed there would be trouble. He took a deep breath and looked at Mrs. Glendower's friendly, faintly worried face. "Is Kelly all right?" he asked. "I mean, is she very sick?"

Mrs. Glendower gave him a puzzled smile. "Why, no, it isn't anything serious, Joe. I think she'll be fine. She had a little headache, that's all."

Joe looked at Sam and David. "Uh . . . maybe you'd better check on her," he suggested to Mrs. Glendower. "Just to be safe, I mean. We'll wait right here."

Mrs. Glendower started to say something, then looked closer at them all. "Well, maybe I'd better," she said uncertainly. She came from behind the counter, wiping her hands on her apron. "I'm sure she's fine, though."

Joe tensed as he watched Mrs. Glendower open the office door.

Mrs. Glendower turned in the doorway. "She isn't here!" she said.

Joe was not surprised. He hurried over, with Sam, David, and Wishbone close behind him. Mrs. Glendower stepped inside the doorway. Joe followed her in and looked around the empty office. "Where was she?" he asked.

"I told her to rest on the sofa," Mrs. Glendower said, pointing to a red-leather couch against the wall under the low window. "I wonder where she went."

Joe walked over and checked the window. It was unlocked, and it slipped up and down easily in its frame. "She must have gone out this way," he said. "The question is: Where? Wishbone!"

The Jack Russell terrier trotted over, ears alert.

Joe patted the sofa. "Where's Kelly, Wishbone? Can you find Kelly?"

"No," Sam said from behind him. "Find Shemp!"

"Great idea," Joe said. "He'll most likely be with her. Find Shemp! Find Shemp, Wishbone! Mrs. Glendower, we'll find Kelly."

Wishbone leaped up onto the sofa and sniffed. Then he went to the window and began pawing at it. Joe opened the window. In a flash, Wishbone leaped outside. He landed on the ground a few feet below.

"Come on!" Joe said.

Wishbone was a short distance away, nose to the ground.

"Good boy! I think he's found the trail," Joe said to his friends.

Joe turned and helped Sam, then David, climb through the open window.

"I think I heard a dog bark!" Sam said. "There goes Wishbone!"

"Hurry," Joe said, his heart pounding. He could hear the barking, too—a series of hoarse, low barks, coming from somewhere near the big screen.

"Smoke!" Sam yelled. "Oh, no—I think I can smell smoke again!"

Joe bounded across the lot, following the white blur that was Wishbone. People sitting in the parked cars turned their attention away from the movie and gave him startled glances as he rushed past. He came to the playground, went past it, and leaped over the low chain fence—placed there to prevent children from wandering off under the screen. Wishbone was already disappearing around the corner of the towering screen.

From behind him, Joe heard Sam gasp for breath as they climbed over the chain. Wondering where David was, Joe turned the corner and stumbled. Once away from the screen's reflected, colorful glare, he was in total darkness.

He knew, though, from the days he had spent helping clean and repair the drive-in that there was a long, low storage building—it was the place where empty boxes, old speakers, and spare lumber were kept. And coming from inside, he heard the low barks of the sheepdog, sounding desperate.

"Wishbone!" Joe yelled. He staggered as someone ran smack into him in the dark.

"Sorry!" Sam said, panting. "Something's burning— I can smell it!"

"So can I!" Joe yelled. "I think it must be coming from the storage building."

Joe and Sam ran around behind the screen, and then Joe heard Sam yelling from close behind him, "Look, Joe—there's the fire!"

A yellow glimmer in the darkness directly ahead suddenly became an angry flame. Joe ran toward it. He coughed. The fire was shooting out from a small, round ventilation window above the storage building door. Wishbone was at the door, leaping and barking frantically.

Joe reached him. He put his hand flat on the door.

"What are you doing?" Sam yelled. "I can hear Shemp inside!"

"I'm checking to see if the fire's right inside the door!" Joe yelled back. The wood beneath his hand was cool. It was safe to open the door. "Stand back!" he said. He tried to turn the knob. It wouldn't budge. "Locked!" he yelled.

From behind the door came a frantic scratching sound. There was no doubt about it—Shemp was trying to break out of the burning building. Joe heaved his shoulder against the door, but it was as solid as a rock. It didn't move.

White light shone in Joe's eyes. David, holding a flashlight, was running toward him, and more people were coming up behind him. Joe started to cough out an explanation, but David shouldered him aside. "I thought we might need some tools, so I borrowed some from the concession building! Get back! Sam, go find a fire extinguisher! Joe, hold the light!"

Joe directed the light toward the doorknob. David opened the tool kit he carried, grabbed a hammer, and swung it hard. He smashed the doorknob once, then again. After the third blow, the knob gave way with a clatter of metal and a crack of wood. Joe stepped back, braced himself, and gave the door a flat-footed kick.

It sprang inward, and a hot rush of smoke billowed out. Joe dropped to his knees and reached through the doorway. He dragged the shaggy shape of Shemp out into the fresh night air. He passed him to David. The inside of the storage shed was orange with the glare of fire. Joe could see that a big stack of cardboard boxes was blazing just inside the door. Shemp gagged and started to struggle, trying to scramble back into the burning building.

"Joe!" David yelled. "I can't hold him!" The big sheepdog pulled away from his grip and bounded back

inside the burning building. To his horror, Joe saw Wishbone dart in after him.

"Stand back, everyone!" Joe barely got out of Wanda's way. She came charging in, holding a fire extinguisher. Just behind her was Mr. Zimmerman, armed with a second one. Wanda turned hers on and began to spray thick white foam on the boxes stacked inside the door. Wishbone barked from somewhere far inside. Mr. Zimmerman joined Wanda in the firefighting effort, and the flames began to die.

Mrs. Glendower came over, carrying a third fire extinguisher.

Joe grabbed it from her. "I'm going to the back!" Joe shouted, coughing. "Wishbone's there!"

"I'll help you!" Mr. Zimmerman said. He joined Joe, and they dashed through the choking smoke.

"Hurry! Hurry!" Wishbone barked urgently, hoping someone would come quickly. A huddled shape lay slumped in the corner, looking lifeless but still breathing. Wishbone's eyes were running, and his nose stung from the acrid smell of smoke, but he would not leave the fallen body.

He heard the hiss of the fire extinguishers, heard Joe's voice. Then Joe and Mr. Zimmerman came ducking through the billowing smoke. They bent and picked up the still figure. "Good boy, Wishbone," Joe said.

Wishbone, his eyes almost blinded by the stinging smoke, followed him out. Joe grabbed him and gave him a hug as soon as he was in the cool open air.

Wishbone tried to lick Joe's face reassuringly. "Shemp? Is Shemp all right? Where's Shemp?"

A low, wheezy "woof" reassured Wishbone.

The Jack Russell terrier pawed at his eyes. He was dimly aware of the murmur of concerned voices. At last his vision cleared. He saw Mrs. Glendower kneeling, saw the body of the rescued person lying on the grass. "Are you all right?" Mrs. Glendower asked the fallen figure.

"Y-yes," the voice answered.

"How did this happen?" Mrs. Glendower asked.

Joe cleared his throat. "Mrs. Glendower," he said, "this is the person who set the other fire—the one at the concession building. The vandal was trying to drive the Moonlight out of business. I think another attempt was made again tonight, but it backfired."

Mrs. Glendower saw the vandal's face. "Oh, no," she said, stunned.

Wishbone felt his heart sink as he heard the sadness and devastation in her voice.

The villain who had tried to ruin the Moonlight was not Mr. Bliss, or anyone else from MegaMall.

It was Kelly Glendower, who lay gasping for breath as the distant scream of sirens grew louder and closer.

Chapter Eleven

Joe, David, Sam, and Wishbone crowded into the drive-in's office with Mrs. Glendower, Wanda, Shemp, and Kelly. Kelly lay on the sofa with a cool, wet washcloth covering her eyes. She was crying.

Someone tapped at the door. Joe opened it to find Mr. Zimmerman there. Behind him stood Mr. Bliss and his assistant, Ms. Corwin.

"May we come in?" Mr. Bliss asked.

"I don't know if there's enough room," Joe said. Still, everyone crowded together a little more, and they all fit inside. Wishbone pressed close to Joe's leg. Joe looked down and noticed that Wishbone's fur was streaked with soot.

"Kelly, I just want to know why," Mrs. Glendower responded. "*Why* did you do it?"

"Oh, Aunt Gladys," said Kelly with a sob, "I did it for you."

"For *me?*" Mrs. Glendower sounded truly puzzled, Joe thought. "What in the world do you mean?"

133

"You shouldn't be struggling financially like this," Kelly said through her sniffles. "I know you don't have a lot of money. You need to sell the land, Aunt Gladys. You won't get a steady income from the Moonlight. I don't want to see you living on the edge of poverty.

"I thought if I vandalized the drive-in, you'd sell it. I also started the fire tonight, but while I was inside the storage building, the wind blew the door shut behind me, and it locked automatically. I couldn't get out, and I didn't have anything to fight the fire with—I thought I was a goner."

Mrs. Glendower looked around the room at everyone, speechless. Finally, she turned back to Kelly. "Living on the edge of poverty? I don't need a lot of money, Kelly. My little pension takes care of everything, even if there isn't much left over. Why, running the Moonlight isn't something I *have* to do. It's something I *want* to do. Who ever told you I was on the brink of poverty—"

Mrs. Glendower turned so suddenly that Joe took a half step back, startled at the anger that had appeared on her face. But she wasn't angry at him. She faced Mr. Bliss directly, staring into his eyes, and she was quivering with fury.

"You!" she exclaimed. "You're behind all this, aren't you! You told my niece all kinds of lies, and in desperation she committed all these awful acts of vandalism. Don't you realize you could have gotten her and others killed?"

Mr. Bliss looked as shocked as Joe felt. "Me? Mrs. Glendower, all I've tried to do is make you a generous offer. I'd never suggest to anyone that they commit an act of violence. I am an honorable businessman, and I have a family myself!"

Kelly sat up on the sofa, taking the washcloth off her eyes. They were red, from both the smoke and her crying. Kelly blinked and said hoarsely, "He's right, Aunt Gladys. He never talked to me." She held out a shaking hand and pointed. "*She* did."

Joe looked at Ms. Corwin, who had a small, icy smile on her face.

"Kelly is obviously upset," the assistant said quickly.

"You did!" Kelly insisted. "You told me that my aunt's only hope was to sell the land to MegaMall. And you said that if enough accidents happened, she'd sell it for sure!" Kelly looked around, tears streaming down her face. "But that's not all," she told the assembled group. "She said that if I couldn't get Aunt Gladys to sell, the MegaMall Corporation would have the land condemned. Then Aunt Gladys would be left without a penny to her name."

"Wait!" Ms. Corwin exclaimed. "Now, I admit that I may have spoken to Kelly once or twice, but—"

Mr. Bliss was staring at her. "You were going to get a big bonus if this deal went through," he said slowly. "Didn't it ever occur to you that Kelly might hurt someone, including herself, trying to arrange an 'accident,' as she calls it? Didn't you even stop to think?"

"I certainly didn't tell her to play with fire!" Ms. Corwin snapped at her boss. "Anyone who would set fire to a drive-in must be crazy, if you ask me. I don't see how anyone can hold me responsible!"

Joe cleared his throat loudly. "When did you talk to Kelly last?"

Ms. Corwin scowled. "I don't have to answer your questions."

"Just yesterday," Kelly said from the sofa. "She called me yesterday and said if the screen was badly damaged, the drive-in would have to close." She lifted her chin and said angrily, "And she *did* mention fire. She said, 'The wooden framework around the screen might catch fire and burn down, for example!' That's what I was trying to do. I didn't want to hurt anyone— and I certainly didn't expect to get trapped in there!"

Mr. Bliss crossed his arms. "So, after you encouraged her to set fire to the concession building and that didn't work out, you suggested to her that the screen could be destroyed? You didn't even warn her of the risk to herself or to others?"

Ms. Corwin's face was very red. She looked away.

Mr. Bliss cleared his throat and looked at her. "Go and wait in the limo, Ms. Corwin."

Ms. Corwin said, "But I did this for—"

"For your bonus. You'd better go," Mr. Bliss said coldly. "I don't think that you'll be sent to jail, which is what should happen, but I can certainly make sure you never hold a position in this business again!"

She stared at him for a moment. Then she turned and hurried away.

Mr. Bliss sighed. "Who figured out that Kelly was causing the trouble?" he asked.

"Joe did," David said at once. "That's why he put us on a stake-out."

"What?" Mrs. Glendower asked, staring at Joe.

Joe felt his face turn hot. "I figured that Kelly had to be involved," he said. "You see, I was reading a mystery book by Ellery Queen, and the big clues in it are psychological ones. When Kelly learned that the Moonlight was going to be brought up to code, she should have been happy, but she wasn't. That's when I realized she had something to hide. Kelly had been here every time the vandal had done something. From little things like cutting the starter cord of the lawn mower and spilling oil in the concession building, to setting the first fire."

"Yes," Kelly admitted. "I did all that."

Joe looked at her. "You sent the anonymous tips to Mr. Penny, too, didn't you?"

Kelly nodded miserably. "Ms. Corwin told me the things I should write about, but I printed the notes and delivered them to Mr. Penny's office. I apologize to all of you. You could have been hurt. Even though Ms. Corwin gave me the ideas, I am responsible for carrying them out."

Joe said, "I didn't have proof that you were behind all this, Kelly. So tonight, Sam, David, and I took turns going to the concession stand to keep an eye on you. When you ended up missing, I knew we had to find you. Wishbone tracked you down by following Shemp."

Kelly smiled at Wishbone and Shemp. "Thank you both. You saved my life."

"I see," Mr. Bliss said. He sighed. "Well, one thing is clear. MegaMall wouldn't be welcome in Oakdale, not after all this bad publicity. Mrs. Glendower, I regretfully withdraw my offer. I'll try to find a site for

MegaMall in another town. I hope there are no hard feelings."

Mrs. Glendower said, "You could not know Ms. Corwin was behind all this. I don't hold you responsible, Mr. Bliss. My niece is responsible. She committed these acts. Kelly could be in serious trouble!"

"She is in serious trouble, but we'll help you find the best lawyer!" Wanda pronounced decisively. "Kelly was misled. I'll stand by her!"

With a nod at Wanda, Mr. Bliss added, "If you need any help—if the police or fire department isn't willing to let Kelly off lightly—please call me. Mrs. Glendower has my card. I know Kelly thought she was acting for the best, even though she was greatly mistaken. Good luck with the Moonlight. I've got to be on my way now. Good night, everyone."

To Joe's surprise, the show was going on. The fire had not been serious enough to cause any damage to the screen, and the audience settled down.

Joe, Wishbone, Sam, and David got back into the Hudson. "I hope Kelly won't have to go to jail," Sam said.

Mr. Zimmerman said, "This is her first offense, and she's a minor. I don't think she will, Sam. She's a young lady who misunderstood what the Moonlight really meant to her aunt. I think Joe's detecting has really put an end to her little stint as a criminal."

"Ellery Queen would be proud of you," Wanda told Joe.

Joe grinned in the dark. "I'm just glad no one was hurt," he said. "It was a challenge to be able to figure out what was going on—but it wasn't so great when I realized that Kelly must have been the one trying to destroy the Moonlight."

"Oh," Mr. Zimmerman said, turning in the front seat. "I almost forgot. After all the excitement, I picked up some snacks, if anyone's still hungry. I have some candy, another tub of popcorn, and— What's this? A package of beef-jerky sticks. Want one, Wishbone?"

Wishbone barked.

A deeper bark answered him from outside the car.

"Shemp!" David said with a laugh.

"Well, there are two pieces of jerky. Think Wishbone and Shemp would like to eat over in front of the screen?"

"I think Wishbone would like to eat *anywhere*," Joe said with a chuckle, opening the car door to let his pal jump out.

Wishbone paused outside the car. He looked back and sensed how happy his buddy Joe was, how content everybody was, to be sitting together, watching a movie roll on the great outdoor screen. He dropped one piece of jerky on the ground, but kept a firm grip on the other.

Shemp ambled over, sniffed the jerky, and all but inhaled it. Wishbone tilted his head, looking at the big dog in the reflected light of the screen. "Now I understand why you were always so nervous and timid. You knew Kelly had some kind of a secret, and you were worried about her. Well, pal, your worries are over. Now you can be a regular happy dog at last. So—I'll race you!"

As they rushed across the grassy playground area just in front of the huge screen, Wishbone heard laughter coming from the cars in the front row. He could recognize Joe's laugh, along with Sam's, David's, and even Wanda's. He did an acrobatic leap right over Shemp, who yipped in surprise. Then Shemp lay on his back, waving his feet in the air, and wriggled in the grass.

More laughter, and Wishbone suddenly realized that the people in the cars weren't amused by the movie on the screen. "Hey! They're watching *us*, Shemp! We're in show business! I've got an idea—let's give 'em a show!"

The two raced, tumbled, and leaped. As for Shemp, well, Wishbone thought that he looked like a normal, healthy, happy dog doing what a dog does best—enjoying life!

That seemed somehow right to Wishbone. There was magic at the Moonlight Drive-In, and Wishbone was seeing it for himself.

About Brad Strickland

Brad Strickland has written nearly thirty books, ranging from suspense and fantasy to science fiction. He enjoyed working on *Drive-In of Doom* because he has fond memories of the drive-ins in Gainesville, Georgia. There were two, the Skyview and the Lanier. He went to both, though his favorite was the Skyview.

Brad remembers the drive-in as a place where the family could watch a movie together and enjoy it, even if the sound was low-fidelity. His greatest adventure at a drive-in happened one night when he and some of his friends were in high school. They saw *It's a Mad Mad Mad Mad World* at the Skyview. Then, when they were ready to leave, they forgot to remove the speaker from their car. Oops! They ripped the speaker right out of the pole it was connected to, blowing out the sound system throughout the drive-in.

Luckily, the owner of the drive-in agreed to let them work there to pay off the expense of repairing the speaker. They spent a couple of hours one Saturday morning picking up trash that people had tossed out of their cars.

In addition to writing, Brad also teaches English at Gainesville College, in Gainesville, Georgia. He and his wife, Barbara, have two children, Jonathan and Amy. They also have an entire household of pets, including two dogs, five cats, and a couple of hyperactive ferrets.

About Thomas E. Fuller

Thomas E. Fuller's first experience at a drive-in was in the 1950s, when his parents took him to see *Moby Dick*—he went along for the ride. The whale was very impressive, however, especially when it looked as if the giant creature were coming right out of the screen. Since then, he has seen a lot of movies in a lot of drive-ins. Years ago it was fun; now he calls it research.

When Thomas isn't writing WISHBONE books with his friend Brad Strickland, he is creating scripts as the head writer for the Atlanta Radio Theatre Company. He also teaches several creative-writing courses at Georgia State University, and works at a Barnes & Noble bookstore.

Thomas lives in a very cluttered blue house in Duluth, Georgia. He and his artist wife, Berta, have four incredibly individualistic children—Edward, Anthony, John, and Christina. Also living with them is a twenty-two-pound orange cat called The General (he appears in *The Treasure of Skeleton Reef*), who wonders when he's going to be featured in another book.

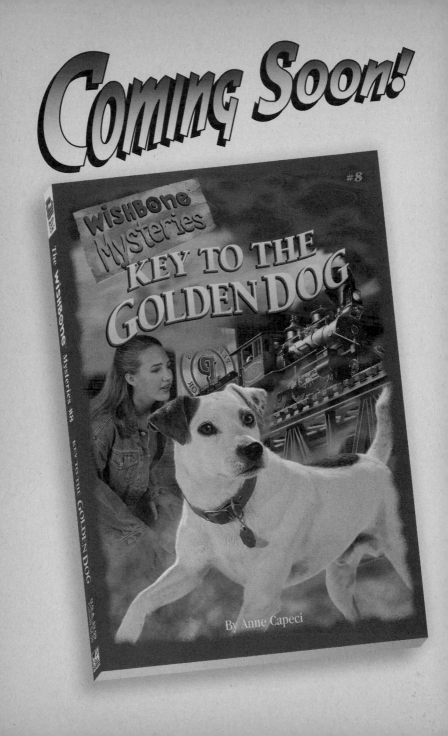